HOW ENDING A RELATIONSHIP CAN BE THE BEST THING FOR YOU

SO YOU'RE IN A BAD RELATIONSHIP? PLAN YOUR
ESCAPE ROUTE!

ALEXANDRA HOFFMAN

CONTENTS

INTRODUCTION

No one has ever said that dating is easy. In fact, it can be one of the most difficult things that you ever have to face. After all, how do you turn a stranger into the love of your life? Everyone you meet and go on a date with isn't going to be 'the one'. There's someone out there for everyone, but it might take you a while to find someone who is the perfect balance for you.

Unfortunately, not everyone is going to be marriage material. Not even everyone will be dating material. There are times when you'll know that you need to get out of a relationship. Then there will be times when you simply don't know whether they're right for you or not. Your friends may be the first ones to notice that there's a problem in the relationship. Once you realize that they're not right for you, the easiest thing is to cut ties and run. Otherwise, you risk your mental and emotional (and sometimes your physical) health by staying in the wrong relationship.

While it would be easy to simply use a checklist when dating, it's usually not that easy. Is he good-looking? Check. Is he smart? Check. Is he kind to me? Check. Do my friends like him? Check. Certain assets are easier to check off than others.

In this book, the goal is to make it easier for you to spot bad relationship types. Rather than providing you with a basic checklist, we'll tell you several stories. This way, you can spot the issues within the stories. You can identify with one couple over another one based on whom you're dating (or whom you've dated in the past or whom you will date in the future). You'll be able to spot a narcissist, a freeloader, or a bully from a mile away by the time you're done with this book.

Once you have read the story, you'll get a therapist's profile view of the couple so that you can see why the relationship is unhealthy. If you're in a similar relationship, you'll find out how to break things off and move forward with your life.

Relationships aren't easy and we understand that. However, there are a number of benefits to being in a relationship when it's healthy and mutually beneficial for both of you. When you both see eye to eye on the important issues, it gives you a person to go through life with. You can share in the ups and downs, potentially start a family, and enjoy the rest of your life with a person.

If a person makes you feel bad about yourself, question your judgment, or lose sight of who you are, you're not in a good relationship. Furthermore, if you aren't on the same path as that person, it may lead to a broken heart. Then you might spend the next few years taking out your disappointment and aggression on other people, and that's not fair to anyone.

We'll show you how you can avoid bad relationships, get out of bad relationships, and find healthier relationships to pursue. You'll be happier and healthier once you're in a relationship where you have found your equal, and we'll show you how to make it happen.

So, you're in a bad relationship? Let us help you plan your escape route.

Not all relationships are meant to last forever. Some people come into our lives to teach us an important and sometimes painful life lessons and then they leave. It's up to us how we use this experience and what we gain from it.

I

I NEED A NEW MAN

"I need a new man." It's the first honest thing you've said to yourself in a while. You know that you're not in the perfect relationship. You know that quite possibly, you deserve better. Now you have to decide what you're going to do about it.

You deserve better. Sometimes, you have to remind yourself of this. Sometimes, you also need your friends to remind you of this.

Bad relationships are bad and often addictive. If you don't get out of them, they can consume you. No relationship is worth being consumed by, especially if it takes your self-worth and self-esteem to all-time lows.

. . .

The guidance shared by marriage counselors can help you to realize that you need a new man. They can even help you to decide a bit more about what kind of man you want and how to know when you've found him.

Once you know that you need a new man, convince yourself of it through and through. It will make it easier to end things with the one you have now. It's the first step to planning your escape route. The longer you stay in a bad relationship, the harder it's going to be to end it.

NOT ALL RELATIONSHIPS ARE GOOD

This may go without saying, but some relationships are inherently toxic. You don't want to stay in a relationship that is bad for you any longer than absolutely necessary. It can damage your heart, your emotions, and your entire spirit. No relationship is worth it if it's breaking you down mentally and emotionally. That's when you know it's time to go.

If you have ever had to justify a relationship, to yourself or to others, it's probably not the healthiest relationship to be in. You shouldn't have to make excuses for why you're with a man. Instead, it should be obvious that the two of you are in love and that everything is going well.

Bad relationships are often addictive. For some addictions, a 12-step program is a necessity. With a bad relationship, the first step is to understand that you're in one. Addictive relationships are dissatisfying and emotionally draining. It may bring you pain in one way or another. You might even be aware of how dysfunctional your relationship is.

You might buy into the conflict again and again because you don't know how to walk away. You make excuses. However, you're not doing yourself any favors. In fact, you're wasting your time, beating yourself down, and losing friendships along the way. If your friends have ever said, "How can you let him treat you that way?" there may be a problem. Furthermore, if you continue to ignore what your friends have to say, they're eventually going to leave you to make your own bad mistakes (over and over again).

If you accept what's happening or pretend it's not happening, you're only making things worse. A bad relationship can lead to anger, anxiety, and depression. None of these things are healthy.

In fact, bad relationships are generally as a result of low self-worth or low self-esteem. Your partner may even be the reason for having such a low self-worth or esteem. They may be verbally or emotionally abusive to a level where you have started believing them. That's not a healthy relationship. That's not what love looks like.

Justifying staying in a bad relationship is dangerous. There are plenty of lies that you may tell yourself, too. Want to know if you're a victim of justifying a bad relationship? See if you've used one of these:

- I can change him over time.
- It's not that bad.
- I don't want to be alone.
- I've invested too much into the relationship.
- I don't want to lose friends over it.
- I don't want to confront him.
- We're too intertwined to be able to leave.
- Dating is too scary.
- I'm not good enough for anyone else.
- I don't want to make him upset.

These are the different lies that we tell ourselves in order to deal with a bad relationship. The problem is, you may love him. You may have a life that is fairly intertwined with him. Whether you live together or not, you may share similar friends. You may work together, go to school with each other, or are involved in various other ways.

You can make all of the justifications that you want. However, bad relationships are bad. The more time you invest, the harder it will be to leave. No matter how hard it is, you owe it to yourself to learn how to walk away.

Staying in a bad relationship is harmful to your health. It can be soul-crushing if you allow it to be. Along with the list of excuses that you have likely used at one point or another, there is an alternative that is considerably more positive. Remembering that excuses are simply excuses, it gives you the strength to move forward.

- You can't change every man that you meet.
- Sometimes, it is that bad.
- Being alone can be healthy.
- Investing time in the wrong relationship is a bad investment.
- Real friends will stay with you even after you leave one of their friends.
- Confrontation is usually not as bad as you think it's going to be.
- Intertwined relationships end all the time.
- Dating can be scary, but it can also be worth it.
- You are good enough for other people.
- Making someone upset by breaking up with them means that they are the one who is unstable, not you.

It may require reminding yourself of these things on a regular basis. You may not be a confrontational person. It is natural to want to avoid drama at all costs. Once you decide that you want to be happy and in a stable relationship, it's worth it to immerse yourself in drama for a short period of time so that you can finally move forward and live your best life.

Learn what a healthy relationship looks like. If all you've ever been in is bad relationships, it may be hard to know what a good one really looks like. In fact, you might assume that 'this is as good as it's going to get'. That's another lie that we tell ourselves because we're scared to take action and go after something that's bigger and better than what we're in now.

. . .

There's a happy medium between the 'happily ever after' romcoms and the 'this will do' mediocre relationship that you're in now.

Take a look at some of your friends or family members for cues of what a real relationship looks like. There should be give and take between the partners. When you ask each member of the partnership separately if they're happy, they say yes and mean it. They don't spend most of their time wrapped up in conflicts or dissatisfaction from one thing or another.

Happiness is available to you. It's out there. You just have to be brave enough to go after it and honest enough to know when you have found it.

2

MARRIAGE COUNSELORS TELL ALL

Marriage counselors are all about trying to make relationships work. They can pick a bad relationship out of a crowd easily. By talking to you for a bit, they can find out whether you and your partner will be able to go the distance or not. They pay attention to things like body language, the level of respect used when talking to each other, goals, and much more.

Marriage counselors suggest that everyone goes through premarital counseling before getting married. It ensures that goals align and that everyone's happy so that the relationship is capable of holding up year after year. Consider it to be an inspection, like you would get when buying a car or a house. A good marriage is going to last longer than either of those things, so it only makes sense to have an inspection.

When you go through premarital counseling, it can be an eye-opening experience. It has you start thinking about the future and how it's going to be with your current partner. It will help you to decide whether you really want to share your life with this person. If the man you're with has a very different outlook on life, compromises may have to be made. In some instances, compromise is out of the question. When this is the case, marriage counselors have to do the difficult thing and identify that it may not be a good idea for the two of you to get married.

Even though you may not be getting ready to say, "I do," just yet, looking at all of the things a marriage counselor will look at during premarital counseling can be a way to decide whether you're in a good relationship or not. If you're questioning whether you need a new man, it's likely that you need to take a good hard look at your relationship.

Different marriage counselors will approach premarital counseling in different ways. Many will use a love languages evaluation to determine if you and your partner are even speaking the same love language. The love languages is a way to improve relationships and was developed by Gary Chapman.

The concept is based on five love languages:

- Words of affirmation
- Gifts
- Acts of service
- Physical touch
- Quality time

Everyone speaks at least one of these languages, though many people speak several. Various quizzes will help you to determine which language is your strongest. If you speak a different language from your partner, it can be as though the two of you are speaking foreign languages to each other. It may allow you some basic communication, but it's not getting the job done to the fullest extent.

If you and your partner speak different love languages, it can be difficult throughout your entire relationship. This is not to say that it will be impossible, but it will be a challenge. This means you have to actively work to speak each other's love languages on a regular basis so that each of you is feeling loved.

For example, if you are strongest in words of affirmation, you want to make sure that you hear words like, "Thank you," and, "I love you." If your partner doesn't say these words on a regular basis, it can make you feel unappreciated and unloved. This doesn't mean that your partner isn't thankful and isn't in love. However, they may have a different love language, such as physical touch. Seeing you and giving you a hug or holding your hand is their way of telling you that they enjoy spending time with you. They enjoy your company and they want to touch you in order to tell you that.

The same can be said about any of the love languages.

Someone may like to give gifts in order to show their love while others may simply want to spend quality time with you, such as taking you out on dates, spending time watching movies with you, or going for a long walk on the beach. Then there are those who believe in acts of service, such as doing special things for you, like cooking a meal, washing the dishes, or taking your car for an oil change.

Knowing how your partner expresses their love is an important step in determining whether you're able to communicate with them or not. Furthermore, you need to know that your partner understands your love language and can speak it fluently in order to give you what you need. Otherwise you are likely going to grow unsatisfied in the relationship.

Different faith-based programs may be used by a marriage counselor as well. Many churches will not marry a couple until they have been given a blessing from a marriage counselor who identifies their compatibility. If a marriage counselor feels that there is poor communication or that the couple is on two different paths in life, they will suggest that the couple doesn't get married. In this case, it can be difficult to find a priest or pastor to provide the nuptials.

Many of the faith-based programs involve asking each partner a series of questions. If the questions cannot be answered or are answered completely differently by each partner, it sends up red flags. This can lead to weeks of counseling in order to sort things out and potentially a recommendation to avoid marriage.

. . .

The questions that are asked by a marriage counselor during premarital counseling should be asked as soon as you start to question whether you need to be in a new relationship or not.

Does the conversation flow easily?

Communication is a big part of any healthy relationship. You need to make sure that the two of you are able to talk about anything and everything. If there are things you feel uncomfortable talking to him about, ask yourself why.

The conversations should flow easily. If the two of you can't get lost in conversation, talking about anything and everything, it's going to be difficult to maintain a relationship for a long period of time. The conversations should never be one-sided either. If one person is doing all of the talking, there's not enough equality in the relationship.

Do you trust everything that he does?

Trust is another pillar in a relationship. Without trust, you have nothing. There may have been things that he has done in the past that have given you reason not to trust him, such as infidelity. If you have chosen to move past an indiscretion, you have to be ready to trust him with your secrets, your worries, and your heart.

· · ·

If you don't feel as though you can trust him, decide whether this is fleeting or if there's something that he can do in order to earn that trust. In the end, if you can't trust him, you have to end the relationship because it will only end up hurting you.

Are you both financially independent?

It's important that each of you is independent of one another financially. If he has a job and you don't, you may lean on him more than what is healthy. If you have a job and he doesn't, it may result in him leaning on you more. In order to move into a good relationship, you have to be financially independent of one another.

While this may not always be the case in your relationship, such as if you two get married and one decides to be a stay-at-home parent after having kids, it needs to be this way in the beginning. Otherwise, it can grow into resentment because of not being able to have your independence. You don't want to question whether they are with you because of the financial situation or out of love.

Can you see yourself growing old with him?

Whether you're 25, 45, or even 65, this is a question you have to ask. Close your eyes and visualize this for a minute. This can be a reality check for you in a lot of ways. Many people don't realize that they're in a relationship just to be in a relationship until they do this check. If you can't see yourself growing old with the man you're with, he's not a permanent fixture in your life.

Similarly, if he can't see himself growing old with you, it's better to know this now. You don't want to be in a relationship that isn't going anywhere, especially if you think it is and he doesn't. It can make your heart hurt for a while, but it's best to identify these things now than investing several more years into the relationship only to find out later on.

Can you see yourself having kids with him?

Too many times, it's easy to get caught up in the feelings of lust instead of love. Younger couples are especially guilty of this. They go down the rabbit hole of lust and romance and forget to think about what it all means. Relationships often lead to marriage and marriage often leads to starting a family. How do you feel about having kids? How do you feel about having kids with the man that you're with?

Many women who are in a healthy relationship get excited about what a good father their husband will become. If you question whether the man you're with will be a good father or not, that says a lot about his character. He may not be treating you the way that you know (perhaps deep down) that you deserve to be treated. If you can't see him as the father of your kids, it's a clear indication that the relationship needs to end.

. . .

Do your religious and political aspects align?

It's hard to be in a relationship if you don't see eye to eye about religion and politics. There are going to come times when you feel one way and your partner feels another. It could become an earth-shattering argument because of very different viewpoints.

While you don't have to agree on everything, agreeing on the big things is important. If you can recognize and appreciate your differences, there's hope. However, if you're Christian and he's an atheist, for example, it can lead to a relational breakdown at one point or another. You should also be able to view each other's differences as different, not wrong. If the two of you argue that one or the other is wrong or childish or stupid for seeing one way versus another, it can result in incompatibility that you can't move past.

It all comes down to knowing whether you're in a healthy relationship or not. You might have started to get the idea that you're not in a fully functional one, and that's okay. It's what you do about it that truly defines you. We're all allowed to make some mistakes in the relationship department from time to time.

Now that you know that you're not with your one true love, what are you going to do about it? We'll help you to develop your escape route, but you have to figure out what kind of man you're in a relationship with. This way, you'll know why the relationship isn't going to work and how it's going to be best to end things.

3

YOU DESERVE BETTER

It's hard to know whether you're in a good relationship or not. Especially if it's been a while since you've dated someone, it can be nice to be involved with anyone. They take you places or they smile at you and you lose all sense of who you are and what you want. At first, it might be your friends telling you that you deserve better.

Don't discount what your friends are telling you. They're not in the relationship. They're looking at things from a bird's eye view. If they see something that's 'not quite right', be sure to listen to them. They may see something that is worth exploring in detail. While not all friends are going to be truthful, your closest ones are looking out for you. Listen to them.

You may start to realize that you're not in the best relationship too. It may start out with him focusing all of his attention on himself. It may be that his actions are setting off alarms in your head. Whatever is going on, it's important that you identify the issues. Some men are capable of changing once you show them the error of their ways. Other men are always going to be that way. It's up to you to know which one is which and get out before they have a chance to cause too much damage.

Think about your endgame. Some relationships are meant to be short. They're fun while they last and then you move on. It might be a fun, innocent summer relationship. It might be a friend whom you decided to move to the next level with only to decide that you were better off friends. It's okay that every relationship doesn't end in marriage. It doesn't have to.

Before you can think about your endgame, it's important to look at the reasons behind dating.

#1 FIND OUT ABOUT THE DIFFERENT TYPES OF PEOPLE OUT THERE

You may want an athletic person who enjoys going to the gym and watching games on Sunday. You might want an intellectual type who spends time buried in a book at a coffee shop. There are all sorts of 'types' out there. It's going to be hard to know what your type is until you put yourself out there and try out a few relationships. The 'type' you think you want may not be right for you at all. However, you won't learn until you actually try it out.

#2 FIND OUT ABOUT YOURSELF

You can learn quite a bit when you're involved in a relationship. You might discover that you are highly opinionated or you lack the ability to make decisions for yourself. If you don't like the person you are when you're with a person or you want to figure out how to change yourself for the better, dating for a little while can be a great social experiment.

It might be a good idea to keep a journal about your dating experiences. Write down what went wrong and why things ended so you know what you're looking for in the next person that you date.

#3 LEARN TO LOVE

Falling in love can be a fun thing to do. However, you need to make sure that you open yourself up for love. If you're too closed off, it will be difficult to let someone in. Although you may find Mr. Right in the dating pool, he may slip away because you aren't ready.

Dating will teach you more about learning to love and letting yourself be loved. Don't be afraid to be vulnerable with someone.

#4 GROW YOUR PERSONAL SKILLS

Learn a few things when you're in the dating phase of a relationship. You'll learn something new with each new date that you go on. It may be to learn to relax, talk more about yourself, talk less about yourself, or to listen a bit more carefully.

You can use some low-risk dating scenarios to grow as a person. Go on some blind dates. Let your friends fix you up. Create a dating profile. Have some fun with dating so that you can grow your skills. This way, when 'the one' comes around, you'll be ready for them.

#5 DATING ISN'T ABOUT COMMITTING TOO FAST

Dating isn't about putting a Band-Aid on a broken heart or jumping into something you're not actually ready for. Especially if you have been in a series of bad relationships, you don't want to jump into something too fast.

Unfortunately, people will often say things like, "Well, I'm not getting any younger," or, "I'm wasting my prime reproductive years." Don't let these excuses cross your mind because they're the wrong reasons for dating and getting involved in a relationship.

Don't commit too fast. Allow a relationship to be fun for a while. You may even want to make a promise to yourself to not get serious for a certain amount of time. It will give you the opportunity to test the waters and know that it's safe to walk away if you're not having fun or it's not the right connection.

#6 DATING ISN'T ABOUT BEING UNHAPPY

Dating is casual. Until you've walked down the aisle and committed your life to another person, it's casual. If you're not happy when you're dating someone, you're not doing it right. Many people date because it's fun, even if they don't want to get into a serious relationship just yet. There's absolutely nothing wrong with that.

Be sure that you're dating in order to find joy. As soon as you stop being happy with dating, it's time to break up with that partner and take a close look at who you are, what you want, and what you need.

Now that you know what dating is, think about your endgame. Everyone's is different, at least at first.

- Is it to have fun?
- Is it to pass the time without being alone?
- Is it to find a potential husband?

There's nothing wrong with any of the scenarios above when it comes to an endgame. And your endgame is likely going to change throughout your life. You might be dating to have some fun now, but eventually, you're likely to date in order to find a potential husband.

Be honest with yourself and the partner that you're with. You don't want to be misled and neither do they.

If you're not focused on your endgame and you're not reaching your goal (such as not having fun or not with a potential husband), you're not in a good dating atmosphere. You owe it to yourself to evaluate your atmosphere from time to time. If the person's not right for you or the endgame has changed, you have to make a move.

. . .

It's only fair. You have to prioritize yourself above anyone else, otherwise you're not being fair to yourself. You need to love you. Date with a purpose, but know that you have the ability to leave that relationship when the purpose is no longer being fulfilled.

You deserve better. It's important to remember. After a series of bad relationships, it may seem that you don't. However, you need to love yourself before you can love anyone else. You deserve the very best in life. By focusing on your self-worth, you're able to avoid making a life-long commitment to the wrong person.

If you know you're not in a good relationship, you deserve better. That's when you may just have to say to yourself, "I need a new man." Once you acknowledge this, you can work to get out of the bad relationship that you're in. This may take some time, but it's worth planning your escape route so that you can move forward with a healthier version of you.

II

WHO ARE YOU IN A RELATIONSHIP WITH?

It's important to know who you're in a relationship with. Sometimes, you don't even remember what drew you to that person in the first place. It may have been mutual friends, an online date, or a chance encounter. Often, being in a new relationship can be blinding. You're so excited that you're in a relationship with someone that you have blinders on to what's really happening.

When you are getting the sneaking suspicion that you might not be in the best relationship, you have to take a closer look as to what's happening in the relationship. This includes identifying who you're in a relationship with. Sure, you know his name. However, how much more do you really know?

. . .

By taking a closer look at the relationship and who you're dating, you can figure out why they're bad for you and what needs to be done in order to end the relationship.

ESTABLISHING THE KIND OF PERSON YOU'RE IN A RELATIONSHIP WITH

You might be in a relationship that isn't balanced. Throughout this book, we're going to cover three main characters:

- The narcissist
- The freeloader
- The bully

As you glimpse over these three, it may be easy to live in denial that you can't possibly be dating one of these types of individuals. However, there's a reason that you're no longer feeling as though they are 'the one', and it's likely because they are in fact one of these characters.

By understanding more about the kind of person you're in a relationship with, you'll see why they're not a good fit for you. You'll get to understand their motives for being in the relationship and why it's better for you to move on, no matter how hard it might be.

Simply reading through a list of characteristics it might be hard for you to spot whom it is that you're dating. After all, it's easier to spot flaws in someone else's relationship than it is in your own. This is why we're going to tell you stories about Molly and three different relationships that she's been in. You'll likely notice situations that you and Molly have both been in. It will be a tell-tale sign that you're not in a relationship with someone who sees you as an equal.

When you know more about the person, you can figure out what makes them tick. You should know why they're in a relationship with you and how it will affect them when you break things off. Preparation is key. Some relationships will be easier to break off than others. Much of this will depend on the type of person you're with, how long the two of you have been seeing each other, and how much your lives are intertwined.

Since all relationships are different, you may also find that you're in a relationship with more than one character. It may be that you're dating a narcissistic bully or a bullying freeloader. Either way, the sooner you know more about the person you're in a relationship with, the easier it will be to see that they aren't worthy of your love.

5

WHY DIFFERENT RELATIONSHIPS HAVE TO BE HANDLED DIFFERENTLY

You need to make sure that you approach the relationship carefully. Otherwise, you could end up getting yourself into even more trouble. You also don't want to feel guilty about ending the relationship. By knowing through and through the kind of relationship you're in, it will ensure that you're aware of why it's time for it to end.

The last thing you want to deal with is sliding backward. Essentially, this means that you don't want to get halfway through the breakup and feel obligated to stay in the relationship because of what the other person is saying or doing. You also don't want to fall for any of their stories as to how they're going to work on things or do better. Especially if you have already given them the opportunity to change, you need to do what's best for you. That means getting out of the relationship once and for all.

When you break up with a narcissist, it's best to end it as

quickly as possible. They'll be fine. They'll just need to find someone else who will admire them. You may have enjoyed being with them, but they were focused on themselves more than you.

When you break up with a freeloader, it needs to be a clean break. Otherwise, it will be a never-ending list of excuses as to why they need to be with you. It all comes down to their inability to take care of themselves. You are not their mother and therefore you're not obligated to take care of them. Realize this, remember this, and end things.

When you break up with a bully, they lose their control of you. It might be necessary to have someone else with you, especially if they have been verbally or physically abusive in the past. Remember why you're breaking up with them and stay strong.

As you can see, each relationship needs a different approach. You don't want to find yourself unprepared for a breakup. Find out who you're dating and take care of what needs to be done. When you find yourself out of the relationship, take a deep breath. You have freed yourself of an unhealthy relationship. You can then focus on how to choose a healthier relationship for the next go around.

III

THE NARCISSIST

Now it's time for you to meet Molly and James. This is a chance to spot some of the problems that Molly is having in this relationship and determine if any of it mirrors problems you're having in your own relationship. After that, we'll analyze the relationship a bit more to provide you with some useful insight.

6

PROFILE: JAMES & MOLLY

olly just graduated from college with her law degree and was glad to be on her own. One of her sorority sisters was eager to play matchmaker. As the two of them were drinking cocktails at a bar close to the college campus, Megan kept pleading her case. She kept talking about one guy in particular, who was good-looking and ambitious.

"Come on, let me set you up with him. He just graduated too. He was in a fraternity with my brother and I think you'll really like him," her sorority sister, Megan, begged. If there was one person Molly trusted more than anyone, it was Megan. They had known each other since freshman year.

"Okay, fine. Make it happen," Molly said. Although she wasn't too pleased about being set up on a blind date, she was excited about meeting someone new. She hadn't done a lot of dating through college because she wanted to focus on her studies. Now that she had graduated, she wanted to start dating a bit more. Plus if Megan said he was a good guy, he must be.

. . .

Everything was set for the date. Molly would meet him at a popular restaurant. She arrived a few minutes before him and hung around the lobby. The moment that James walked into the restaurant, she knew she was going to like him. He was tall, with dark hair and a radiant smile. He saw her, smiled, and smoothed back his hair. He introduced himself and let the hostess take them back to the table.

There was a bit of an awkward silence at first so Molly asked, "So, what are you doing now that college is over?"

James spent the rest of the night telling her all about the modeling career that he was offered. He had spent the past week in New York on a photoshoot with a high-end fashion magazine. James said that the magazine would be coming out the next month and he'd make sure that she got a copy. Molly laughed and said that it sounded like a lot of fun.

After the restaurant, Molly suggested going to the beach but James didn't want to get sand in his shoes. He suggested taking a walk through the mall so that he could check out some of the latest fashions. He told Molly that it would be great to get her input on what she thought was stylish. She agreed. She found James charming and enjoyed listening to him talk about fashion designers she had never heard of.

James held her hand and walked through the mall with her. At one point, he stopped and slid his hand in her hair, tucking it behind her ear. She got goosebumps when he did it and smiled at him. He smiled down at her, too.

. . .

It wasn't long after that the two became inseparable.

"Why don't you join me for my photoshoot in New York this weekend?" James offered. "I'd love to have someone there rooting for me."

"Sure, would that be okay?" Molly asked, eager to see James in action.

"Absolutely. Those assistants around there do anything I ask of them," James said.

Molly told Megan about her trip to New York. "See, I told you he's amazing. I'm glad that it's working out for the two of you." Molly was happy about things too. Her friend was happy about being a successful matchmaker too.

When Molly arrived at the airport in New York, she waited at the baggage terminal for James. She texted him, wondering where he was. There was no response. Finally, she called him. "Hey, where are you?"

"Oh," James said. "I didn't realize you had landed. I'm in the middle of a shoot, so I'll send an assistant on the set for you." Before Molly could ask any questions, he had hung up.

"Okay, that's no problem," Molly said to herself. She was a small-town girl and there was nothing small-town about New York City. She wheeled her suitcase over to the benches along the wall and sat down.

About an hour later, a mousy brunette came over to Molly. "Hi, umm, are you Molly Tanner?" It was the assistant who James had sent over to get Molly and take her over to the set.

"That's me," Molly said, grabbing her suitcase and

following the girl. The ride to the set was quiet, with Molly not knowing what to say to the assistant or about James.

James made a big fuss when she arrived, apologizing that he wasn't there. He took her around to meet all of the photographers and assistants. By the time he was done introducing her to everyone, she had forgotten almost everyone's names.

"You're good here for a while, babe?" James asked.

Molly nodded. "Go, be fabulous," she smiled. James smiled back at her and gave her a thumbs up. She was left to sit there and cheer him on for over two hours. Every now and then, he would look at her and give her another thumbs up. She returned it, letting him know that she was okay and that he could continue.

Once he was done, he scooped her up and gave her a kiss in front of the entire staff. She shied away a little bit, but he didn't care. He wanted everyone to know that this was his girl.

James snapped his fingers at one of the assistants. "You made that reservation I told you to, right?"

The assistant blinked for a second. "I... ummm... they were booked for tonight. They said that they're booked three months out. I made a reservation at a different place that you're going to love."

James rolled his eyes and looked at Molly. "I'm so sorry, it's really hard to find good help around here." He said it loud enough for the assistant to hear every word.

Molly shook her head. "I'm sure wherever we go will be great." She turned her attention to the assistant. "Thank you for making reservations. I bet the place you chose is amazing."

James didn't say anything else to the assistant. Rather, he

grabbed Molly's hand, gave a wave to the photographer, and walked to the elevator. "I'm so glad to be done for the day. Tomorrow is an evening shoot, so we have all tonight and most of the day tomorrow to do some sightseeing. There are a few places I've wanted to go."

"That sounds great. I've been wanting to see a few places, too," Molly gushed, excited that she was finally in New York City.

"Of course. You've never been to New York City. It's a good thing you're dating me. I'll make sure that you get to see more of the world. The restaurant is one of those places that is crawling with celebrities, so that should be exciting," James said.

"I can't wait." Molly couldn't, either. She'd never dated anyone like James before. He was good-looking, ambitious, and always ready to pamper her with gifts and expensive dinners.

A few days later, Molly flew back home. James would be back in a few more days. He said he had big plans for the two of them. She couldn't wait to find out what it was going to be, but she promised she'd be patient.

James was making a big deal out of something. He called all of his friends and told her to have all of her friends come out to a restaurant. He was ready to make an announcement.

"You don't think he's going to pop the question, do you?" one of Molly's friends asked.

"I can't imagine that he'd do that. It's way too early in our relationship," Molly said. If he did pop the question, though, Molly was running through what she'd actually say. As she ran through the scenarios in her head about what it could be about, she decided that if he did ask, she would say yes.

"What could it be, then?" her friend asked. Molly

shrugged. She was excited to find out what it would be, whatever it was.

That night at the restaurant, James showed up in a limousine. He got out and made his way to the front of the crowd. "Where's my girl? Molly, come on up here."

Molly blushed but made her way up to the front. James thanked everyone for coming out. "So, I guess everyone wants to know what the big news is, huh?" Everyone cheered. "I'm leaving for LA next week. I've got a part in a movie!"

Everyone cheered again. Molly could feel her brow furrow. Why wouldn't he have told her first? Why did he need to make such a big deal out of this? She pushed her thoughts away, knowing that he was excited to be heading to Hollywood. She was confident that if she had landed a role for a movie, she would make a big deal out of things, too.

Everyone came up to congratulate him. She gave him a kiss on his cheek and walked over to her friends. A few of them were shaking their heads at her.

"So, no ring," one of her friends said. Their disappointment was clear.

"No ring," Molly confirmed. "But I wasn't expecting one either." She really wasn't ready to settle down just yet. Maybe down the road, but definitely not right now. She wasn't completely convinced that James was the marrying type, but they had plenty of time to find those things out.

Later that night, Molly was at James' house. "I can't believe you're headed to LA next week."

"I know, it's crazy, right?" James went on to explain that someone had shared some of the photos from the photoshoot with a casting director that they knew and, as they say, the rest was history.

"Does this mean we're not going to see much of each other for a while?" Molly asked. She didn't want to lose her man, especially now that he was going to start getting famous.

"I'll be out there for about three months. They're setting me up with a trailer on set. Once I get settled, I'll fly you out for a week. How does that sound?"

"That would be amazing," Molly smiled. She was thrilled that a boyfriend was willing to spend that kind of money. All of her previous boyfriends were in high school and barely had enough money to pay for a movie. Being flown out to LA, and to a movie set no less, was amazing.

"Then it's set. After all, I need to have my biggest fan out on the set with me," he chuckled. "Maybe you can set up a fan site for me." She laughed. However, he was more serious than she realized at the time.

Molly couldn't believe that James was having such luck with his career. She graduated at the same time that he did, but she wasn't nearly as successful. She was enjoying the summer and would soon start an internship at a law firm. James hadn't asked about any of that yet, so she was eager to share her plans. After all, she would be starting at the law firm in less than six weeks.

Time seemed to fly by and before she realized it, she was hopping a plane to Los Angeles. To avoid a problem like the last time she flew to meet James, she decided to get a taxi. He offered to pay for it, but she didn't want him to think she was too needy. She was looking for an equal partner after all, and didn't want to be dead weight.

Her name was on the list at security. The taxi left her off at the gate and she was ushered to the set via golf cart by a security guy whose name tag read 'Andy'.

Andy was telling her all about the movie and how exciting it was. It was a shoot 'em up kind of movie with a lot of explosives and special effects. It wasn't really her type of movie, but she tried her best to fake enthusiasm. He pulled up to the back of the set. "Here you are, sweetheart."

"Thanks, Andy." Just like that, Molly was left on her own to try to find James.

A production assistant came up to her to ask who she was and why she was there. "I'm here to see James Narsee."

"Oh, he's such a good actor. A little snooty, but he's doing well around here. Follow me."

Molly wondered what they meant about being snooty but decided to ignore it. She was in Hollywood and everything around her was so exciting.

As soon as she heard, "That's a wrap," she started to look out for James. A number of people strode off the set and her heart skipped a beat as she noticed a few high-profile celebrities.

"Molly, my girl!" he yelled, causing half the studio to turn and look at her. She waved awkwardly and walked over to him. "How are you?"

Before Molly could answer, he had her hand in his and was practically dragging her all over the set, explaining what different things did and who different people were.

"Can you stop introducing me as your biggest fan? It's embarrassing," Molly said after being introduced that way for the fifth time in a row.

"I'm just teasing you. Lighten up. Besides, they all know that you're my girlfriend. You're hot like I am and hot people are meant to be together," he chuckled.

Molly smiled, happy that he noticed that she was attractive. "So what's the plan tonight?" Molly asked, looking to lighten up the mood.

"I need your help running lines in my trailer. Then there's a new club opening up that I got us on the list for. My agent said that I should be there to help my image. Plus you make pretty good arm candy. We just have to do something about some hotter clothes for you," James explained.

Molly looked down at herself. "What's wrong with my clothes?"

"They're just not Hollywood. Don't worry about it. We're on break for the rest of today, so we can go shopping. There's a stylist at a store nearby who will get you taken care of. My agent sent me over there the first day I arrived. And now look at me," James said.

Molly nodded. "Okay, well I guess that could be fun. Apparently I have to look good to be a movie star's girlfriend." She was feeding into his ego, which she knew he liked.

"That's right. You're dating a movie star. Wait until we get to walk the red carpet together," James said.

The red carpet wasn't something Molly had thought about until James said it. She didn't know just how big his part was, but if it was a Hollywood blockbuster, there probably would be a red carpet walk. It was exciting.

A production assistant walked by and James snapped his fingers. The assistant stopped and looked at him. "What's the name of that store that Carlos sends everyone to?"

The assistant said the name and kept walking. James rolled his eyes. "That guy is always so rude."

Molly pointed out that James was the one to snap at him. "He's used to that. He's just a production assistant." Molly shook her head and walked with James to the front of the studios to wait for an Uber.

After an evening of shopping and running lines, Molly and James were off to the grand opening of a new club. Molly's dress was too short and her heels were too high, but James thought that she looked 'LA sexy', as if that was supposed to make it all okay.

James identified his name and was ushered into the club. The security guard placed his hand out to stop Molly. "Sorry, there's no plus-one."

"What?" James asked. "I was told that there would be a plus-one. This is unacceptable." The security guard shrugged. He didn't know who James was, which only made James more upset over the situation.

Molly teetered on her heels, uncomfortable about standing outside of the club. She didn't want to be there, but she was happy to do it for James. Plus she really did want to find out about this club and brag to her friends about being able to go.

"Okay, well, I need you to wait here. I'll call my manager

to get this straightened out, but I need to go in. They're expecting me," James said.

Before Molly could argue, he was in the club. Molly smiled at the security guard who looked down at her, rolled his eyes, and shook his head. Molly stepped to the side with a frown on her face while he started checking off other people on the list and letting them into the club.

After an hour of waiting outside, Molly texted.

"Just a few more minutes," was the only response that she got from James.

Another hour and Molly was pissed. She was tired and she was frustrated from being given dirty looks from the security guards. She didn't even have a hotel room because she was staying in James' trailer. She called an Uber and headed to a restaurant for something to eat. Then she texted James to let him know where she was.

Another full hour passed by before she heard from him. First, it was a text to tell her to stay where she was. Then he showed up at the restaurant. "How could you just leave?" He came into the restaurant, yelling from the front door. The restaurant wasn't that busy, but heads were definitely turning.

"It was over an hour," Molly said in her defense. She said it quietly, looking around the restaurant. She didn't want to make this into a bigger issue than it needed to be.

"I have a reputation to protect. How does that look for me that my date just leaves? I have to leave this great opportunity to go and chase you down so that I don't look like a crappy boyfriend. Do you know what kind of social opportunity you just cost me? You're so insensitive sometimes."

. . .

Molly sat there in the booth of the restaurant with her mouth hanging open. How could he say that to her? He must have seen her face and the scene that he was causing. He waved to a couple of people as if to shoo them away. He sat next to her, cuddled her close, and whispered into her ear.

"Let's head back to my trailer. I think we're just over-whelmed by what's happening."

Molly nodded and paid her bill. James was glad to be out of the restaurant to avoid any kind of scene. He wasn't known in Hollywood yet, but he knew it was only a matter of time before the paparazzi would show up. Scenes like tonight couldn't happen again, and he would see to it that they wouldn't.

"Do you think we can try another club tomorrow?" James asked, once they were back in the trailer.

Molly let out a sigh. "Will I be on the list this time?" She was hurt and upset that he hadn't bothered to check the last time. If he was going to insist on her being at his side, she didn't want to get dressed up for nothing again. Especially since she had to wear 'LA clothes', she wanted it to be for something.

"I promise," James said. "I need a plus-one and my manager knows that. Right now, you're good for my image." He smiled and wrapped his arm around her as though he had said nothing wrong.

"Right now?" Molly asked, hoping that he wasn't going to dump her when he got famous.

"That's not what I meant. You know what I mean," James said, waving it off. He knew that she was pretty and smart. He also knew that he needed to keep a girlfriend next to him for a while because that's what his manager told him to do.

. . .

True to his word, James made sure that Molly was on the list the next night at the club.

"Oh, you're with someone else tonight?" a reporter asked James as they made their way into the club.

James froze for a moment. Molly looked at him and back at the reporter.

The reporter saw what was happening and pressed on. "This brunette was not your date yesterday. Last night you were dancing for hours with a busty blonde."

"She was just a girl," James said, trying to dismiss the issue.

"And this is your girlfriend?" the reporter asked.

"A close friend," James said and pushed their way through to the club.

"You were dancing with another girl last night? That's why you never came out to get me?" Molly asked.

"Oh, stop it. I have to put on a show. I'm a celebrity now and you have to respect that," James said. He didn't try to explain anything. He was simply telling Molly how it was going to be from then on.

Molly had a big decision to make, but she didn't want to. She was starting to fall in love with James. Being with another girl at the club though, while she waited outside, was not okay.

James mentioned that he wanted to fly her out again around the first week of September. Molly told him about the law internship that she was starting. He frowned and said he didn't understand how she could do that to him.

"What are you talking about? I have a career, too," she explained. James didn't seem to want to hear about it. She felt bad that she was letting him down. She said she'd see what she could do. That's how they left it when she left to fly back home.

When she was talking to her friends about LA, they looked as though she was nuts. "You can't leave your dreams of being an attorney behind."

"Well, James needs me right now," Molly explained to them. She understood that James was alone in a new city and having someone at his side helped him to get through everything.

"He's using you. All you are is arm candy to him," one of her friends explained. Some of her other friends shared similar thoughts about the relationship.

Molly shook her head. "You're wrong. He's always been extremely generous to me."

That's when Molly realized that she might not have everything that she wanted. She had to decide if she was going to sacrifice her career to be with James. That's what it would take to be with him. He needed her there in LA. Her career path needed her to take the internship her sorority had helped her to snag. She was in an uncomfortable position.

Molly had come to a crossroads in her relationship. She already knew that he wasn't the right one for her. She never came first. The whole reason that he seemed to want to date her was that she made for good arm candy. He didn't take the time to get to know who she was or what she wanted in the world. That's why it came as such a shock to him that she wasn't able to fly out to LA in September. He had assumed that she'd be there at his beck and call instead of asking her about her life. Had he taken the time to get to know her, he would have known about the internship and how important it was to her.

Unfortunately, deciding to break up with him was harder for Molly than it was for James. She was afraid to give up on a relationship that could really be something. She liked the fantasy that he painted for her, especially with him being in a movie.

In the end, Molly listened to her friends. She listened to her heart. She called James and broke up with him over the phone since he was still in LA and she was back home.

"We need to talk," Molly explained when he picked up the phone.

"Sure, what about?" he asked.

Molly knew that there was no easy way to do this. "I don't think we should see each other anymore." Before she had a chance to go into detail, he interrupted.

"You're breaking up with me?" James asked, sounding shocked. Clearly he had never been the one to be broken up with. It wasn't shocking, though. He was probably a heart-breaker all throughout college.

"I think it's best for both of us," Molly tried to explain. "You're all the way on the other coast."

"You don't know what you're giving up," James said and hung up on her. He didn't try to fight for her or convince her to stick around. Instead, he figured that since he was an up-and-coming movie star, he would be able to find someone else in no time.

. . .

Molly let her mouth hang open. She wanted a bit more closure than what James had given her. Unfortunately, that wasn't going to happen. She was shocked that James was so childish, hanging up on her.

After a few months of not talking to James or hearing anything about him, she found out that his movie had been released. Unfortunately, the director had cut him from the scenes he was in, so he never got his moment on the big screen. Somehow, this made Molly more excited than she could possibly admit.

7

RELATIONSHIP COMMENTARY

James was a narcissist. Often it was hard for Molly to see what he really was because he was a nice guy 'most of the time'. This is often the problem with narcissistic personalities. They're self-centered and need everyone to prioritize them; however, they aren't necessarily jerks in the average sense of the word. James did love Molly in his own way, which is why he flew her to New York and Los Angeles. He paid for things as a nice gesture in return for her being at his beck and call. It made him look good, so he covered the costs.

The biggest problem in the relationship was that the only one James would ever make number one was himself. Molly was never going to be placed on a pedestal because there was no room for her next to James' ego. Molly would have had to lose herself in order to be with James. She had a strong enough personality to realize that. She wasn't ready to sacrifice who she was just to be with him.

. . .

There were plenty of scenarios throughout the story where James showed off his true colors. The very first encounter with Molly in the restaurant revolved solely around him. He talked about all that he was doing with his modeling career. While Molly found it interesting, he didn't ask about her and her plans at all. In future relationships, Molly would be able to use this as a way to spot a narcissist early on.

Essentially, if you're in a relationship with someone and they never ask about you, your day, or your hopes and dreams, it doesn't mean that they don't care. It just means that it's not something that they think about because they're so focused on themselves.

There are other situations where James lets his true colors shine, too:

- Introducing Molly to everyone so that the spotlight was on him.
- Making a big deal about his movie deal in front of his friends and hers.
- Identifying her as his 'biggest fan'.
- Expecting her to wait for him while he went into the club.
- Making Molly jealous with the other girl in the club.
- Expecting her to drop everything for his time in LA.

When Molly left the club to go to the restaurant, James had to leave the spotlight. He was caught in-between doing the right thing and getting his moment in the spotlight. While he chose to do the right thing by going to her, he went into a narcissistic rage in the process. Walking into a restaurant yelling at her is not normal behavior. She was embarrassed by it and James didn't really apologize for his actions.

Normal relationships are about balance. There are going to be times where someone in the relationship is having a good day, whether it's a promotion or something else. It is the other person's responsibility for showing that they care. However, it goes both ways. The person who is up in the world today needs to be ready to support their partner when the roles are reversed.

Molly would never be prioritized. She wasn't in a relationship with someone who would be ready to support her through the ups and the downs. Had Molly continued the relationship with James, she would have needed to ask some serious questions before she got married to him. Imagine what the wedding would look like. James would likely be taking the spotlight and deciding who would be in attendance and what she would wear. This isn't because James wouldn't want Molly to have the perfect wedding but he would need to control how it would look for him. He would need to make sure the wedding was suitable for him and his image that he was so desperate to protect.

Kids would also likely be difficult with a narcissist like James. They would need to learn to perform their 'roles' as the perfect children. They would be celebrated when they performed as they needed to as opposed to for their own victories. This makes it hard for children of narcissists to grow up with a balanced outlook on life because they don't know how to do things that make themselves happy.

Now that Molly has dated a narcissist, she will know how to identify one in the future. She'll look for cues such as whether they ask about her, how they introduce her to their friends, and how they respond to things going on in her life.

Unless a narcissist gets the professional therapy that they need, it's hard for them to be in a relationship because there's no healthy balance.

When you're dating a narcissist, you have to look closely for the signs. Sometimes they're not as obvious as you think they should be. This is why it's so hard to get out of a bad relationship. You assume that you're in a relationship with a good guy. You become blind to the issues because you like him and you don't want to move away from the status quo. However, narcissists are never going to put you first. You may end up losing yourself in order to make him happy.

IV

THE FREELOADER

Molly is now onto a new relationship. Discover how Molly and Blake meet and how their relationship works in order to identify the various flaws. You may notice that there are similar issues within your current relationship. After the story, we'll go over the relationship to provide a bit more insight that can be beneficial.

8

PROFILE: BLAKE & MOLLY

Molly and a few of her friends from the law firm she was interning at would go to a local bar almost every Friday night. It was their way of letting off some steam while having some fun. Molly couldn't help but notice a tall, blond-haired man who was a bartender. He would flirt with her a little bit when he dropped off her drinks. He introduced himself as Blake. Whenever she would come in, he would make a point of being in her section.

Every week, this would go on. Blake's smile would make her dizzy. He finally got up the courage to ask for her phone number. Her friends urged her to pursue the bartender to find out what he was like. He wasn't a narcissist. That she could already see. She decided to throw caution to the wind one Friday night and typed her name and number into his phone.

. . .

True to his word, he texted the next day. "Are you free for dinner tonight?"

Molly couldn't help but smile at the idea of going out with the handsome bartender. "Okay."

He didn't have a car, so he asked if they could meet at a local restaurant. She agreed and he texted her the address of the place just in case.

When she arrived by Uber, Blake was already standing outside of the restaurant. "Hi," she smiled at him.

He smiled back. "You look great."

"Thanks," she said and followed through the door that he held open for her. The restaurant wasn't anything special, but it was busy.

"We have reservations," Blake said, approaching the host stand. It was only a few minutes before they were following the server to a table.

"Have you been here before?" Blake asked, after the server had stopped by for drink orders.

Molly shook her head. "Not yet. It's been on my list. What's good here?"

Blake recommended the burgers. Once the server returned, that's what they both ordered. Then they went back and forth talking about all of the reasons they loved the city. They loved the cold winters and being able to go just about anywhere in order to people-watch. Molly was surprised to learn that they had so much in common.

"How long have you been working at the bar?" Molly asked.

Blake took a bite of his burger at the same time she asked and they both laughed. He held up a finger to tell her to hold on a minute. "About three months. I like it there, but what I really want to do is pursue my art."

"You're an artist?" Molly asked.

Blake nodded. "I work with oils on canvas. A friend of mine owns a gallery a few blocks away and told me that once I get enough pieces that he'll let me have a show there."

"That's amazing," Molly said.

"What about you? I see you come in with your friends all dressed up every week," Blake commented.

Molly laughed. "Yeah, it's a whole lot of work. I'm interning at a law office. About a year ago, I graduated with my degree. Now I have to intern as a way of proving that I know what I'm talking about while I work to take my bar exam."

"Wow, so you're really smart," Blake smiled.

The conversation was easy between them all throughout dinner. The server dropped off the check and Blake immediately grabbed it. He reached into his back pocket and then looked over at Molly.

"This is really embarrassing, but I forgot my wallet," Blake said.

Molly told him it was no problem and she covered the check for the two of them. Blake promised to pay her back. For Molly, it wasn't that big of a deal. She wanted a relationship that was even. She didn't expect every man to buy every meal. She was happy to do it and told him that the next dinner would be on him.

Only it wasn't. The two were eager to go out on another date and made plans for the following week. Molly should have known something was up when he wasn't at the bar when she went in with her friends. She figured she would just ask him about it on Saturday when they had plans to go out to another restaurant across town.

"I got fired," Blake explained. Apparently there were too many bartenders at the bar and the place wasn't as busy as it used to be. He was one of the most recent to be hired, so it only made sense that he was one of the first to be fired.

"What are you going to do now?" Molly asked.

Blake didn't really seem to have an answer. He said he would find another restaurant to bartend at. He was staying at a friend's house, so as long as he had the rent by the end of the month, he wasn't too concerned. However, it also meant that he didn't have enough money to cover dinner.

Molly was a little upset that she didn't know this going into the date. While she had the money to pay for the date, she didn't want to be the one to pay all the time. She would have suggested that they do something else, like maybe go to her apartment where she could have cooked. She told him that she didn't mind though and he thanked her with that smile that melted her heart.

After dinner, the two of them took a walk through the city. It was a full moon, and they commented on how beautiful it was. Then Blake told Molly how beautiful she was. He took that opportunity to kiss her for the first time. She admitted to her friends the next day that the kiss made her swoon.

.   .   .

"He's really good-looking," one friend commented. Her other friends chimed in to agree. Molly smiled, knowing that she had a guy who was kind, cared about her thoughts and opinions, and made her friends a little jealous because he was so handsome.

Soon enough, Blake and Molly had been dating for nearly three months. Blake, true to his word, found another restaurant to bartend at. He had bought a few dinners for Molly, to return all the ones that she had bought. This helped to balance things out for Molly.

She saw his art, too. He made a point of taking her over to his friend's house, where he was still crashing. The art was creative, but it wasn't really something that Molly understood. For her, it looked like a bunch of paint splashed onto the canvas. However, she smiled and supported him. She wasn't an art critic, so she had no idea whether it was good or not.

Molly asked Blake a few times about whether he had plans to get a place of his own. "Yeah, I mean, at some point. My friend doesn't mind me crashing at his place. He gets help with his rent money and I get a place to stay."

"You don't want more privacy?" she asked. She loved having her own apartment because of the privacy it offered. She couldn't imagine staying at someone's apartment, even if it was a friend. She figured she'd last a few days at most, certainly not weeks.

Blake shrugged. "I guess it's not a big deal. Besides, when we want privacy, we just go to your place," he smiled.

. . .

Molly supposed that was true. She understood that everyone was different and that's what made it possible to have good relationships. The chemistry between her and Blake was undeniable. Her friends commented about that on more than one occasion. Blake was always smiling at her, even when he didn't think she was looking. Her friends said that they wanted a guy who would look at them like he looked at Molly.

One weekend, Molly was excited to be off. This seemed to be like the longest weekend ever. She was glad to be getting together with Blake, too. He was on his way over, and she was going to cook for him for the first time.

When he showed up, he had a few bags with him. Molly's eyebrows arched as she looked at him. Blake frowned.

"What's going on?" Molly asked.

"My friend kicked me out because I didn't pay him the full rent that I owed him. And I just lost my job," Blake explained.

It was Molly's turn to frown. "Well, come in. So, how did you lose your job this time?"

Blake shrugged. "I don't know. The manager just kept cutting my hours. When I asked him about it today, he fired me altogether." He moved his bags into the living room and looked at Molly. "I was hoping I could stay here for like a week until I can get back on my feet."

Molly took a deep breath. They'd only been dating for about

three months. Moving in together was a big step, but she didn't want to leave him on the street either.

Blake could sense her hesitation. "I promise it will be for a week, two weeks max."

Molly nodded. "Okay, two weeks max." She then muttered something about hoping that her parents didn't find out that she was living with a guy.

The two of them had a good time throughout the rest of the night. She made spaghetti and meatballs and put Blake in charge of a few different things. He had to open the bottle of wine and set the table. She stayed in the kitchen, stirring the marinara sauce and draining the pasta.

"These might be the best meatballs ever," Blake commented.

Molly smiled. "I made them myself."

Blake continued to compliment her on her cooking. After curling up on the couch to watch a movie, it was time to go to bed.

This was when Molly realized that things were about to get awkward. Normally she would kiss him goodnight and he'd leave to go home. However, this was now his home, too. At least temporarily, she thought. She reached into the junk drawer in the kitchen to pull out a spare key for him, too.

They got ready for bed, brushed teeth side by side, and climbed into bed. Blake rolled over and gave Molly a kiss on the cheek before rolling over to his side of the bed. Molly lay awake for a few minutes, reveling in the feeling. She kinda liked having someone to kiss her goodnight. It was a little strange and it would take getting used to, but she did indeed enjoy having Blake staying with her.

The next morning, she told her friends at work about what had transpired.

"You let him move in with you?" one friend asked.

"Temporarily. It's no big deal," Molly explained.

"It's a big deal. You have to make sure he doesn't take advantage of you. I had a cousin who let a boy move in for a while and he never left. Just be careful," her friend said.

Molly agreed but didn't see what the big deal was. They had been dating for a while and Blake needed a place to stay for a week or so until he could bounce back.

When she got home, Blake was already there. He greeted her with a kiss and told her that he was working on dinner.

"It smells delicious. You went grocery shopping?" Molly asked.

"Yeah," Blake said. "I noticed you had a shopping list taped to your laptop. I placed the order using that grocery app thing that you have."

Molly wasn't sure exactly what he was saying. "So, you bought the groceries that were on my list with my account?" That would mean that she paid for the groceries and everything had been delivered right to her apartment. While that was something she was planning to do anyway, she hadn't expected Blake to help himself to her computer, or her bank account for that matter.

"Yeah, I was trying to do you a favor. I added a few things on there that I needed, too," Blake said and smiled. Before Molly could argue, he went back into the kitchen to stir the mashed potatoes.

Molly followed in after him. "What are we having?"

"I made meatloaf and mashed potatoes," he said.

Molly nodded. A few minutes later, dinner was being served. They took a seat across from each other at her dinette set. She took a few bites and let him know it was good. "Did you find a job today?"

Blake shook his head. "Not yet. But my buddy said that he's having a mixed artist show next month and that I could put some stuff out. Hopefully I can sell a few pieces."

"That's great news," Molly smiled. She had no idea how much art like that would sell for, but she was hoping that it would be enough to get Blake back on his feet. "You're still looking for a job, though, right?"

"Yeah, yeah, of course," Blake said and smiled at her.

After dinner, she helped him get everything cleaned up. Then the two of them watched some TV and went to bed. It seemed to be the routine that they had naturally fallen into. Molly was excited by all of it because it was new. She also felt like she was getting to know Blake a lot better. Blake said that he was enjoying living with her, too, even if it was temporary.

Nearly a week went by when Blake stopped into her office. The receptionist came into the room where Molly was working with some of the other interns on a big project. "Molly? Your boyfriend is here. He says he needs to see you."

Molly excused herself and went over to Blake. "Hey, what's up?" she asked.

"Umm, I needed to borrow twenty bucks. I have an interview all the way on the other side of town and need money for an Uber," he explained.

"Oh, umm, okay. Just hang on a minute." Molly went over to her desk to get a twenty to take to him.

"Thanks," he said and kissed her on the cheek. He was out before she knew it.

When she went back in, one of her friends, a colleague, asked what was going on. Molly told her why he had stopped by.

"Tell me you didn't give him the money," her friend said.

Molly rolled her eyes. "Of course I gave it to him."

"Girl, you have to be careful that he's not playing you," her friend advised.

Molly dismissed her friend. She knew that Blake was struggling. She was happy to help him. After all, he was a nice guy. Everyone falls on hard times periodically and if she could help, she would.

When Molly got home, Blake was still out. "Maybe that means he's having a good job interview," she thought to herself. She went in to make the bed and take care of a few other things. She noticed that he had a new pair of sneakers on his side of the bed. They must have been in the suitcase that he brought with him. He hadn't had enough money to spend that kind of money on shoes since moving in.

Blake rushed in through the door, nearly giving Molly a heart attack. "You're never going to guess what happened," he said, spinning her around and kissing her.

"What? What?" she asked excitedly.

"I got the job. It's at a really top-notch restaurant on the other side of town. The tips should be killer," he explained.

"That's amazing!" Molly said.

"We should celebrate tonight," Blake announced. "What do you say we go to that restaurant we first went to?"

Molly nodded, though she also realized that she'd have to pay since he didn't start the job yet. She knew it was only a matter of days now before he would be able to start paying for things on his own again. Plus she couldn't wait to get out and have some fun with him. Although she enjoyed living together, she didn't want to miss out on date nights.

Three days later and Blake was set to move out. "I talked to one of my friends and he's going to let me crash there. I know I promised that I'd be out within two weeks," Blake said as they were having dinner.

Molly didn't know how to explain to him that she wanted him to stay. She liked the partnership that they had created. She was able to come home after work to find dinner in the works. Sometimes he had even done laundry. Plus Blake was working a regular job again and was bringing in money. He even bought dinner the other night, which was a nice treat.

"What's the matter?" Blake asked.

"I guess I don't want you to move," Molly said.

"You like having me around?" Blake asked.

Molly nodded. "I really do. I mean, my parents would kill me if they found out that I was living with a guy before marriage, but I really have enjoyed these past few weeks."

"Me, too." Blake knew that he could probably continue to stay with Molly, especially if he told her he wanted to. Plus she had never even asked for a dime toward rent. The friend that he was moving in with was demanding five hundred dollars a month. Staying with Molly would be a lot cheaper. "I could stay if you really wanted me to."

Molly perked up at this idea. "I really would. You like living with me? I mean, like, you're happy here?"

"Of course," Blake said and he gave her a kiss across the table. "I'll tell my friend later that I decided to stay here."

"Good," Molly said.

The rest of the evening was spent unpacking Blake's clothes and making room for a few more of his things throughout the apartment. Molly wanted to make sure that he had plenty of space to call his own. She was excited about taking the 'official' next stage in their relationship.

Blake's art show was coming up the next weekend. Molly had invited everyone from the law firm and passed out flyers with Blake all over town. While his art wasn't alone at the show, it would be an opportunity to take a step toward his dream of being an artist. Plus he could possibly sell quite a few pieces.

Unfortunately, the art show didn't go as either of them had planned. While the art show was mobbed with people, no one bought Blake's paintings. Several of Molly's co-workers commented to her that they didn't 'get' his artwork. No one could understand the statement that Blake was making with his art, which only frustrated Blake.

. . .

He promised that the next show would be different. He had already set up an easel in front of the window of Molly's living room to work on his next piece. Paint was all over the place and Molly hoped that it was easy enough to clean so that she could get her deposit back.

"I think I might have to get a second job," Molly said over drinks with her friends the following Friday night.

"What? Why?" one friend asked.

Molly shrugged. "The apartment is expensive. Food is expensive. And Blake has been talking about going on vacation with me at the end of the month." They had talked about going on a cruise, which sounded amazing.

"Is he paying for anything right now?" her friend asked.

Molly shook her head. "Not right now because he's trying to get everything up and running. He just started at his new job a few weeks ago. His art show didn't go very well, either."

All of her friends stared at her. "You're making excuses," one said.

"I'm not. I really love him. Besides, no man is perfect. So what if I have to support him a little bit? If things were reversed, he'd do the same for me," Molly explained.

"Would he, though?" a friend asked. "I mean, you guys have only known each other for a few months. He's been mooching off of you since you met. Literally since the two of you met, you've paid for almost everything."

Molly got upset with her friends. Most of them were single, so they didn't understand. She didn't care about buying dinner and things every now and again. If he needed a little time to get going, she would give it to him. She paid for her drinks and left, not wanting to talk to anyone. She just wanted to go home to Blake. He was supposed to be working late, so she figured she'd watch a romcom before he came in.

When she opened the door to her apartment, Blake was on the couch eating popcorn. "Hey, you're home!" he greeted her.

"Hey, I thought you were on a closing shift tonight?" Molly asked.

Blake set the popcorn down. "Yeah, about that. I quit earlier today."

"What?" Molly asked. She was already worried about money and him not bringing in money again wasn't going to help matters.

"I figured I need the time to work on my art right now. If I'm ever going to sell something, I need diversity in my portfolio," he explained. "Besides, you're covering rent so it's not like I need the income."

The way he said it made her pause. She was afraid that her friends may have been right. However, she was still hopeful that this could be fixed.

"Listen, Blake," Molly explained, "I'm happy to help but I can't support you entirely."

Blake nodded. He said that he understood. He said that he'd work on getting a job 'soon' in order to bring in the money that was needed. In the next breath, he was talking about the cruise again. Molly didn't want to be the sole funder of the cruise, especially if he wasn't going to bring in any money toward it.

· · ·

Molly left the apartment to call her friend Megan. She needed advice on what to do.

"You already know what you need to do," her friend said. Molly didn't know. Her friend told her she needed to kick him out. "You have to get your life back on track. He's wasting your money and your time."

"But I love him," Molly insisted. "What am I supposed to do? Just kick him out? Where will he go?"

"That's not your concern," Megan said. "Seriously, he was a mooch before you met him. He was doing just fine. He'll find someone else to mooch off of."

Molly knew her friend was right. When she returned to the apartment, she saw Blake at the canvas. He had a lot more paint near him than the last time. She asked him about it and he said that he had emptied most of his savings at the art store to get supplies.

That's when she knew she had to do something. Rather than pitching in toward rent, he used it on art supplies. That wasn't okay.

"We need to talk," Molly said. Because of the tone that she used, Blake set his paintbrush down and sat on the couch next to her. Molly explained that she couldn't continue to support him. She told him that he needed to move out.

"You asked me to stay," Blake reminded her. "I missed out on the chance to stay with my friend because you wanted me here."

Molly bit her lip because this was harder than she thought it was going to be. "I know. I'm sorry, but you're not even trying to maintain a job. It's not fair for me to support you like this when we haven't even known each other that long."

Blake argued his way to try to stay a few more days. "Just a week. You'll see how we can make this work."

Molly shook her head. "No. A week will turn into a month." Molly was able to hold strong. "You have to leave tonight."

Blake yelled at her. When Molly didn't respond, he finally began packing up his things. Molly sat on the couch in tears as he did, not knowing what to say to him. She wanted to tell him to forget it and that everything would be okay. However, she continued to cry. He said goodbye to her on the way out and that she'd regret doing this. She hoped that he was wrong about that part.

Molly's friends were right. Once Blake was out of the house, she was able to get her life back on track. They even planned a cruise together, with each of them paying their own way. She never did find out whatever became of Blake, though she figured that was for the best.

9

RELATIONSHIP COMMENTARY

Blake was a freeloader. While he meant well with his relationship with Molly, he was taking advantage of her every step of the way. She really liked him. Her friends thought he was good-looking, too, so she liked him even more because of the image he was able to help her with.

Freeloaders are looking for someone else to take care of their problems. They don't have a plan for how they're going to improve their financial status because they're always looking for the 'next big thing' to come along. For Blake, he was so focused on how his art was his ticket to financial freedom that he didn't see how it was affecting his relationship with Molly or his ability to support himself.

Blake also used manipulation in order to make it look like it was Molly's idea for him to stay with her. No one will ever know whether Blake was telling the truth about whether he really had plans to move in with a friend or not. He was counting on the relationship that he had built with Molly for her to feel bad. This is often the problem with freeloaders. They weave themselves into the life of another person so closely that it's hard for the other person to resist their charms.

There were plenty of signs that Blake was using Molly:

- Forgetting his wallet on the first date.
- His inability to hold down a job.
- His lackadaisical attitude about getting a new job.
- Not paying any rent money to Molly.
- Spending money on foolish things (sneakers, art supplies) instead of being financially responsible.
- Planning a vacation that Molly would have to pay for.

Molly's friends had already told her that she needed to be careful of Blake. They saw that she was spending all of her money to keep the relationship going. However, Molly had been hurt before. She didn't want to end up alone. She saw Blake as a nice guy who had fallen on hard times. She didn't want to be the one to end things just because he wasn't working and he couldn't maintain a job. She was hopeful that someone would do the same thing for her if the roles were reversed.

The biggest problem with a freeloader like Blake is that the situation never gets better. He had no intention of getting a 'real' job. He also didn't seem to have enough artistic talent to make it as an artist, which is evident by him not selling any pieces at the art show. Rather than that being a reality check for him, he quit his job and spent all his remaining money on art supplies in order to focus on his art.

He felt he had the ability to do that because Molly was footing the bill for everything. He didn't respect her enough to feel as though they needed to have an equal partnership.

There are times where one partner will fall on hard times. However, there are also ways of knowing whether it's a temporary situation where the person has every intention of fixing things or not. Freeloaders aren't going to fix anything. They move from one temporary situation to the next because they lack responsibility or the care to be responsible.

Healthy relationships are about respect. Blake didn't respect Molly enough to make sure that she was okay with spending her money. He ordered groceries using her grocery account with her credit card without even asking. He made assumptions that it would be okay. With doing that so early on in the relationship, it was disrespectful.

Furthermore, Molly and Blake weren't married. She didn't owe him anything at that time. This is where it's important to remember that dating is all about determining whether someone is a suitable mate prior to getting into a permanent situation with them. She didn't have the means to support him because she was talking about having to get a second job. Blake hardly showed that he was motivated to earn money for himself, even though he was perfectly capable of doing so. It was simply easier for him to rely on Molly. He was taking advantage of her generosity.

Once married, Molly and Blake would be responsible for supporting one another. If she lost her job, it would be his job to provide support and vice versa. However, prior to marriage, there's no reason for Molly to continue to support him. Blake was even ready to watch Molly get another job just so that she could continue paying for everything. This should have set off a number of red flags for her. It was setting off red flags for her friends.

Molly would have ended up with big problems had she married a freeloader like Blake. She'd be forced to work two jobs in order to make ends meet. Meanwhile, she'd be married to someone who was so busy chasing his dreams that he didn't have time to work and earn a living. She'd be stressed while he'd be living his best life. Kids too in that situation would be problematic. The kids would likely spend more time in daycare than anything else because Mom was working all the time and Dad was too busy working on his art or chasing his 'next big thing'.

When you're dating a freeloader, you have to look closely for the signs. They're not always as obvious as you wish that they were. This is why you may find yourself in a bad relationship. You may get so carried away that you're in a relationship that you don't realize that he's using you. You become oblivious to the bigger problems because you don't want to break things off and face single life again. With a freeloader, there will never be a healthy balance of responsibility. Particularly when you're in the dating phase, there's no reason for you to feel as though you have to support another adult who is capable of supporting themselves.

V

THE BULLY

Molly has dusted herself off and moved on to another relationship. Explore how Molly and Ryan meet and how their relationship builds. Find the various flaws of the relationship to see how Ryan is a bully. There may be some similarities within a relationship that you're currently involved in. After the story, we'll talk about the relationship in detail so that you can see why ending things was the best move for Molly.

10

PROFILE: RYAN & MOLLY

Molly had been working hard at the law firm. She went from being an intern to passing the bar. That's when her law firm decided to hire her full-time as a lawyer. She'd been single for a while and some of the other lawyers at the firm had been trying to set her up.

"I'm really not looking for anything serious right now," Molly said to one of the clerks, Faith, who she works with at the county.

"I'm not talking about setting you up with just anyone. My brother is a prosecutor with the county," Faith said. "I really think the two of you would hit it off."

Molly thought about it for a while. She never had much luck with people setting her up, but she did like the fact that Faith's brother was a prosecutor. It meant that he had a good job and understood the time commitment of her job. Plus

Faith was an attractive woman so she hoped that good looks ran in the family. "Okay, one date."

Faith smiled. "Great. I'll have him give you a call. I already have your number. His name is Ryan."

"Okay," Molly said and she gathered up her bag to head back to the office.

Two days had passed and she hadn't heard from Ryan. When she was back in court, the prosecutor on the case was named Ryan. He was tall, with dark hair, a little stubble on his chin, and a navy suit that looked like it was tailor-made for him. She wondered if this was the same Ryan that Faith was trying to set her up with.

She decided to approach him. "Hi, I wanted to introduce myself," she said, walking up to him.

He smiled as if he already knew who she was. "Molly, I know. You're taking the lead on this case, right?"

She stumbled a little. "Um, yes. I was just wondering if you had a sister named Faith?"

Ryan nodded. "Yes. She also gave me your number to call you."

"You haven't though," Molly said, feeling as though she was being rejected.

"I haven't yet," Ryan emphasized. "I can't date the opposing counsel. Until this case is closed, we can't have any kind of personal relationship."

Molly felt her cheeks burning red. Duh, she should have known that. "Right, of course," she said, straightening her skirt.

"I do intend to call you, though," Ryan said and winked.

Molly smiled and returned to her side of the courtroom. That explained a lot. She liked his level of confidence and how he carried himself. He had already done his research on her. He seemed very sure of himself that they would have a 'personal relationship' even though they had never even spoken before. She couldn't help but be in an upbeat mood for the rest of the day.

It took a week to close up the case that Molly was working on. Within a few hours of leaving the courtroom that day, her phone rang. It was an unknown number, which made her a little excited at the thought of who it might be.

"Hello?" she answered the phone.

"Would you like to get drinks to celebrate your victory?"

"Ryan?" she asked, hoping that she wasn't about to embarrass herself.

There was a chuckle on the other end of the line. "So, you were anticipating my call. Does that mean that you'll meet for drinks?" Ryan asked.

Molly smiled. "Sure. Where would you like to meet?"

"Do you know where Augusta's is?" Ryan asked.

Molly said that she did. It was on the other end of town, but she didn't mind taking a drive. It was supposed to be one of the top bars in the city with an incredible view. She hadn't been there personally but had heard plenty of good things about it.

. . .

When she walked in, he was already at the bar. He stood to greet her, giving her a kiss on the cheek. "It's nice to formally meet you, Molly," Ryan said and he gestured for her to take a stool next to him. "I ordered you a Cosmopolitan."

"Oh, thank you so much. It's nice to get a win under my belt early on," she smiled.

"You won't be going up against me, so you should have plenty of luck," Ryan countered.

"I won't?" she asked.

Ryan shook his head. "I don't think it would be a good way to start off dating, do you?"

Molly smiled. "So, that's what we're doing here? Dating?"

Ryan shrugged. "We're two intelligent people. I don't see any reason why we shouldn't be together. I've actually had my eye on you for quite some time."

"You have?" Molly asked, taking a sip of her Cosmo.

"I have. I usually get what I want, too," Ryan said and he placed his hand on her knee.

Just like that, the two of them fell into a comfortable rhythm of being around each other. They were an instant item and everyone in the courts and her law firm knew that they were dating. They had to file documents in order to allow them to date, stating that they would never take a case that involved the other one working. This would avoid any favoritism or conflicts of interest for their clients, too.

"Let's go away this weekend," Ryan said one afternoon, catching up to her in the halls of the courthouse.

"Oooh, that sounds like fun. Where to?" Molly asked.

Ryan thought for a minute. "I'm not sure yet. Where do you want to go?"

"Maybe Cape Cod?"

Ryan nodded. "I'll look into it and book something." He

gave her a kiss and headed to the other side of the court-house for a briefing.

Molly returned to her office to get some paperwork done. A weekend alone with Ryan sounded exciting. She was eager to be in a relationship that was about balance. After some of her past relationships, she was a little hesitant. However, Ryan was capable of running his own life. He also seemed genuinely interested in her and what she wanted to accomplish.

Just as she was gathering up her stuff to leave for the night, she received a text from Ryan. "Portland, Maine, here we come." Molly smiled, excited for the chance to get away. However, she also remembered talking about Cape Cod. Maybe there wasn't any availability out there for the weekend.

"Sounds good," she texted back, adding a smiley face for good measure.

Both of them had a lot of caseloads in front of them, so they didn't talk much throughout the week. This is one of the reasons why Molly liked Ryan so much. He understood her inability to go out often during the week because of her work.

Friday came around and he was planning to pick her up at three so that they could get on the road early. She texted to let him know that she was running a little late. He told her it wasn't a problem and that he'd be there when she was ready.

.   .   .

By five, they were finally on the road toward Maine. "We're probably going to miss the dinner reservations now," Ryan said as he drove.

"I'm sorry," Molly said. "I didn't realize that you had made any."

"Of course you wouldn't have. That's what I get for being thoughtful," Ryan said but he didn't make eye contact with her when he said it.

Molly sat back in the seat and took a deep breath. They were both exhausted and she didn't want to fight. She decided to go for an easier conversation. "Did you see the political debate last night? I caught the tail end before I went to bed."

Molly soon realized that the two of them were on different sides of the political fence. She had just assumed that he had the same leanings as she did.

"You're too young to realize that you're wrong," Ryan said. "Let's see how you feel about these same issues when you mature a bit."

"Excuse me?" Molly asked, shocked that he would go there.

"Relax, I'm kidding. But you're clearly not informed enough about the issues to talk about them in an intelligent way," Ryan said.

Molly huffed and decided to drop the conversation. They were both tired. She was also hungry because she had skipped lunch. She turned on the radio to break up the silence between them.

Ryan didn't bother changing the station. Instead he said, "We should be there in about an hour."

Molly nodded and relaxed in the seat.

An hour later, Ryan pulled up to a beautiful bed and breakfast on the coast with a lighthouse in the background.

"It's beautiful," Molly commented.

"It definitely is. Much better than the places I could find around the Cape. We'll enjoy the privacy here. Let's hurry. We can still make our dinner reservations," Ryan said, getting out of the car.

The restaurant was within walking distance of the bed and breakfast. As soon as they were settled in the room, Molly freshened up her lipstick and changed her shoes.

"Ready?" Ryan asked, holding out his arm.

Molly smiled and grabbed his arm. "Ready."

At the restaurant, Ryan ordered a bottle of red wine.

"I'm more of a white wine kind of girl," Molly commented.

"That's because you haven't had the right kind of red," Ryan said, dismissing her thoughts on the subject altogether.

Dinner was good. Molly thought the wine was just 'okay' but didn't want to start anything with Ryan. It was late by the time they got back to the room. She was ready to kick off her shoes and go to bed.

"Did you want to go for a walk around the property?" Ryan asked.

Molly shook her head. "I'm exhausted. Can we do that in the morning?"

Ryan sighed. "Sure." She could tell he wanted to say something else, but she didn't push. With the amount of work she had done this week, she just wanted to let her head hit the pillow. Tomorrow would be fun. The two of them had talked over dinner about what to do and decided on a boat tour as well as hitting a place for chowder. It sounded like a relaxing weekend and Molly was excited to do it with Ryan.

Most of the weekend went without a hitch. They held hands, they kissed, and they spend the entire weekend sightseeing all over Portland. It was relaxing. There was one brief incident where Ryan yelled because they had to go back to the bed and breakfast when Molly's heel broke. It wasn't something that she had expected to happen. Plus he yelled loud enough for a number of heads to turn. Molly brought plenty of shoes, though, so they were back out sightseeing in no time at all.

"You must deal with a lot," Molly said as they drove back to the city.

"What do you mean?" Ryan asked.

Molly tried to choose her words carefully. "As a prosecutor, it's a stressful job."

"Nothing I can't handle," Ryan said.

Molly smiled. "Well, I know you can handle it. I'm just saying that it must be a lot at times."

Ryan nodded but didn't say much else. He wasn't one to talk about his feelings a lot and Molly came to understand this. She felt that his yelling and carrying on sometimes was because of the stress of his job. She hoped that weekends like this would be enough to help him relax a bit.

A few weeks went by and she received an envelope on her desk. It was an invitation to her law firm's holiday party. She was supposed to take a 'plus-one.' She smiled, knowing that she would ask Ryan to accompany her.

"I'm excited about this holiday party," Molly said to some of her co-workers in the breakroom.

"You know why they tell you to bring a plus-one, right?" James, one of the lawyers who was in line to be partner, asked.

Molly and a few of the others shook their heads.

"The partners want to know that you have a life outside of the office. Those who are married or are in strong relationships are more likely to make partner faster," James explained.

"Really?" Molly asked.

James nodded.

Molly thought that was interesting. She'd only been working as a lawyer for about a year, but partner was definitely something she wanted at some point. Having Ryan, a prosecutor for the county, as her date, would help her to look good. She was eager to impress the partners. She sent off a text to Ryan immediately to invite him to the party. She knew that he had a variety of social engagements this time of year, many that she was invited to with him, and wanted to make sure he got the date on the calendar. There was no way that she was showing up to the party alone.

"Sounds good," he texted back shortly after.

. . .

Ryan and Molly met for dinner that night. Over dinner, they worked on getting their calendars aligned. He had a few parties he had to go to where it would be better if he had a date. The only thing Molly had was the holiday party. There were also a few dates for the new year that she shared with Ryan, including a retreat that the firm had mandated for everyone. It was easy for Molly to see a future with Ryan, so it only seemed right to share things that were happening at least six weeks away.

It seemed like legal cases always increased around the holidays. Ryan and Molly did a lot of texting back and forth and met up for coffee several mornings, but they hadn't had a chance to spend a lot of quality time with one another. Instead, they settled for a quick kiss as they passed each other in the courthouse.

Finally it was the night of the holiday party. Ryan had booked a town car to take them to the party, which was being held at an upscale venue downtown. Molly had bought a new dress especially for the occasion.

"You look great," Ryan said, holding the door open for her.

"Thanks," she blushed. "I'm really excited about the party."

Ryan looked down at her heels. "They're not going to break, are they? You're kind of a klutz sometimes."

Molly shook her head and gave him a punch on the shoulder. "No. They're not as high as the ones I wore in Portland. Besides, I'm not a klutz."

Ryan rolled his eyes at her but held out his arm for her to hold. "As long as you can manage dancing with me later," he said and gave her hand a pat.

"We can definitely make that happen," Molly smiled.

The two spent the next hour shaking hands with her partners and being introduced to top clients of the firm. She saw
a few of her partners' eyebrows raise when she introduced
Ryan as being a prosecutor with the county. Ryan didn't
disappoint, either, with talking about his job and his relationship with Molly. He did well with her crowd.

"Partner might be coming sooner than you hoped," Ryan
whispered to her when they were on the dance floor.

"Really? What makes you say that?" Molly asked, giddy at
the possibility.

"Well, I carry a bit of clout in these circles. It makes your
firm look better to have a better relationship with the courts.
Becoming more than just a lawyer would be good for you,
too," Ryan said.

"Just a lawyer is still a great job," Molly reminded him.

"For now," Ryan said. "But you can't expect to be just a
lawyer forever. Partner is what you need to strive for. Sooner
rather than later, too. It's better for my image, too."

Molly nodded. She knew that there were a lot of cutthroat
lawyers at her firm. They didn't get to where they were
because of being nice. If she wanted to make partner, she
would have to play by a new set of rules. Maybe Ryan could
be of help there.

A week after the party, Ryan was out of town for work.
Molly met up with some of her friends at their favorite bar.

"When are we going to get to meet him?" one of her
friends asked. Molly had been dating Ryan for almost six

months but hadn't introduced him to her friends yet. They both seemed so busy that it was hard to coordinate something.

"Soon, I promise," Molly said.

"I don't know how you do it," another friend said.

"What do you mean?" Molly asked.

Her friend explained that it was a lot to be a lawyer and have a new relationship. Molly said it was better that Ryan had a time-demanding job, too, because he understood. She also confessed that there were times that she had thought about ending things with him so that she could concentrate on moving up in the firm.

It wasn't until a few days later that Molly got a chance to see Ryan after his business trip. He talked about how he was able to attend some really great workshops while he was on the other coast. He asked about drinks with her friends. She said it went really well and mentioned the conversation that they had had about maintaining a work-life balance.

"You're not going to break up with me," Ryan said.

Molly laughed, thinking that he was joking. "I might." She had no intention of breaking up with him right now, but she felt she had the right to do so at her discretion.

"You will not break up with me. You'd regret it," Ryan said.

This time, Molly didn't laugh. There was something about the way he said it through clenched teeth that scared her.

"I love you more than anyone else could love you," Ryan

said, walking over and wrapping his arm around her shoulders. "We make a great couple. Everyone here sees that."

Molly nodded. She'd actually been told that on more than one occasion. Even one of the law partners said that they made a great couple when they were at the holiday party.

"If you don't think that you see enough of me, why don't you move in?" Ryan asked.

Molly's mouth hung open. "What?"

Ryan smiled. "You heard me. Move in. You could get rid of your apartment. Mine's bigger and better anyway. Plus we'd sleep in the same bed every night, guaranteeing seeing more of each other."

"Can I think about it?" Molly said, shocked that he was inviting her to move in. It was a big step in their relationship and one that she didn't want to take lightly.

"Sure. Just don't wait too long or I'm going to move on to some other beautiful woman," Ryan said.

"What?"

"Relax, I'm kidding," Ryan chuckled. Molly was quick to get defensive about different things and Ryan didn't understand that. He wanted to have the perfect life and the perfect wife would help in that area. He just needed to get Molly to understand that he was helping her.

Molly texted her friends about his suggestion to move in. A few of them told her to wait while the others encouraged her to try. As one pointed out, "You don't really know someone until you are able to live with them." Molly agreed.

The next day, as she was walking down the hall in the courthouse, Ryan was just stepping out of a courtroom. "Hey," he said, grabbing her arm. "Did you have a chance to think about my question?"

Molly smiled. "Yes."

"Yes, you thought about it or yes, you'll move in with me?" Ryan asked.

"Yes to both."

"Wonderful. We'll work on getting you moved this weekend," Ryan said. "It should be easy since your furniture doesn't have to go."

Before Molly could ask what he meant, he kissed her on the cheek and explained that he was running late for a meeting.

The weekend was fast approaching and Molly was getting more and more excited. She packed boxes each night, making sure that she had her books and other things. Her apartment was highly sought-after because of the view, so the complex told her that she could break her lease without a fee. It all seemed perfect.

Faith, Ryan's brother and Molly's friend, stopped Molly in the courthouse. "You guys are moving in together?" she squealed. "I told you that the two of you would work out. You're going to become my sister-in-law in no time."

Molly smiled but got nervous. Moving in with Ryan was one thing. Getting married was another. She liked Ryan a lot but she also felt uneasy about the way that he would tease her sometimes. She shook her head to clear her thoughts and went about the rest of her day.

. . .

Moving in with Ryan was easier than she would have thought. He had a U-Haul pull up to her apartment with a few people who were hired to do all of the heavy lifting. He then took photos of her furniture so that it could be sold online.

"All of my furniture?" Molly asked. There were a few pieces she really liked.

Ryan shrugged. "You don't need that furniture. It's outdated, so I don't even know why you like it. My apartment has all of the furniture we need." She figured he was right. There was no need for two bed frames or two couches. Besides, the money from selling the furniture could be used for a vacation. One of her partners had a place in St. Barts that they had offered to her if she wanted to get away for a long weekend with Ryan.

"See, we fit together," Ryan said. "Everyone thinks that we make the perfect couple."

After living with Ryan for a few months, Molly's friends made comments to her when they were finally able to go out with her. "You've changed," they all said in one way or another.

"What do you mean?" Molly asked, concerned that her friends were going to say something bad about Ryan.

"You seem more hesitant. You wait for all of us to order before you do," one of her friends said.

"And you second-guess what you are going to wear," another friend said.

Molly shrugged. "Ryan helps me make decisions. I don't see anything wrong with that."

Her friends exchanged glances but didn't say anything. Molly knew that part of what they were doing was being cautious for her. She also knew many of them didn't have successful relationships. They were likely jealous because she had such a good thing going with Ryan.

"I'm glad that you live with me," Ryan said when she got home.

"Me too," she smiled, kicking off her shoes by the door.

"This way, I know you're mine. You can't be with anyone else," he smiled and pulled her close to him on the couch.

Another week went by and Molly's friends were commenting about Ryan again. "We need to meet him," they declared.

Molly decided to invite Ryan out to the bar with her on Friday so that they could all meet him.

"I don't think you should even be spending time with them. They don't do anything but complain about their lives," Ryan commented.

"That's not fair. They've been friends of mine for years," Molly said.

Ryan shook his head. "Fine. We'll go make an appearance but only for one drink. Then we have more important things to do."

Molly nodded, happy that Ryan was agreeing to go meet her friends.

Friday could have gone better. First, Molly had to show up to the bar without Ryan. When she texted him, he claimed that he had forgotten and that he was on his way.

Molly was sipping a Martini when Ryan showed up. "Getting hammered with the girls?" he asked.

· · ·

She laughed it off. "Of course not. Everyone, this is Ryan." She went around and named everyone so that Ryan could know who she was spending time with. "I'm glad you could make it," she smiled, giving him a kiss on the cheek.

"If I don't nail this case, it's your fault. I had to leave a pile of paperwork at the office to come to meet your little friends," he said.

"I'm so sorry," Molly apologized.

"Wait, what are you apologizing for?" one of her friends butted into the conversation.

Molly's cheeks turned red. "Nothing, don't worry about it."

"I have to get back to the office, so I'm just going to have one drink," Ryan said.

Molly nodded. He ordered a drink and was very short with his answers when Molly's friends asked about what he did and what he liked to do. True to his word, once the drink was done, he said goodbye.

"You'll be back at my place before I get home?" Ryan asked.

Molly nodded and waved.

Her friends were shaking their heads.

"Oh, stop. He's just stressed right now," she defended Ryan.

"He's changing you," one friend said.

"And not for the better," another added.

Molly explained to them that while the relationship wasn't perfect, it was just fine. She also told them how hard it would be to end things 'even if she wanted to' because of working together. "Even though we don't take the same cases, I'd see him in the courtroom every day. There's no way that I'd want to deal with that," Molly said.

Her friends didn't like what they were hearing. They couldn't understand why she'd settle rather than end things. Molly knew why, though. She loved Ryan. Their lives had become intertwined. Sure, he could be a little critical at times. However, she also knew that like her, he had a stressful job.

The following week, Molly got the wake-up call that she needed. She was coming out of one courtroom and Ryan was coming out of another. She went to give him a kiss and he raised his voice. "I cannot believe that you let me be talked into meeting your friends. I lost this huge case because of that. Your friends are a distraction." He huffed off down the hall before she could say anything.

Derek, a lawyer from another firm, one she went to law school with, came over to her. "Are you okay?" he asked.

Molly nodded. "Yeah, umm, he's just stressed."

Derek shook his head. "No, I'm sorry. I know that this isn't my business but that's not a man who's stressed. He's verbally abusive."

"You don't understand," Molly said.

"I do," Derek said. "My sister dated a guy just like him." He reached into his pocket. "Listen, if you ever want to know what it's like to date a nice guy, call me." He handed her his business card and gave her shoulder a squeeze. "I'll see you later."

. . .

Molly went back to the office to think everything over. Could Derek be right? Was that what her friends were trying to say, too? She didn't want to leave Ryan. She hated being single. However, she didn't like how he would raise his voice and constantly talk down to her. She was scared of breaking up with him, though. That's when she realized that there really was a problem. She shouldn't be scared of breaking up with someone. She just had to figure out how to do it carefully.

Molly decided to call one of her close friends to see if she could move in temporarily. When her friend found out that Molly was going to leave Ryan, she was happy to help. She also suggested that Molly break up with him publicly so that she wasn't at risk of being hurt.

Molly called Ryan and asked him to meet her at a restaurant right after work. She said it was to get drinks and talk. He agreed.

He sat at the bar next to her. "Hey, what's up?"

Molly frowned and took a deep breath. "We need to break up. I don't think it's a healthy relationship anymore."

"Absolutely not," Ryan said, getting louder than was necessary.

"Excuse me?" Molly asked.

"No. We're not breaking up," Ryan said, even louder this time.

Molly shook her head. "It's not just your decision. This is part of the problem."

"This is ridiculous. You're listening to your friends instead of your heart. You love me," Ryan said.

Molly shook her head again. "I don't know what to say. This is ending. I'll be working on getting everything out of the apartment tomorrow."

As Ryan started to yell louder about her not moving out, the bartender asked him to quieten down.

"This isn't the place to do this," Molly said. "Think about what I said. Maybe we can talk in a week when things calm down."

Ryan shook his head and stormed off. Molly sat at the bar crying, nearly hysterically. She texted a friend to come to pick her up. She knew the breakup would be hard but didn't know it would be quite this hard.

Molly waited until she knew Ryan would be at work the next day. She went into the apartment and cleared out her things. Then she locked the door behind her, happy to be done with this chapter of her life.

The next time Molly saw Ryan was in a courtroom. She had given his apartment key to his sister, Faith. It wasn't long after that she heard that Ryan had taken a job at the next county over, where he most likely found another victim.

11

RELATIONSHIP COMMENTARY

Ryan was a bully. While he never hit Molly, he ruled the relationship with fear. She worked with him, too, so she was fearful of ending the relationship on a bad note.

There were a number of times when Molly felt as though she had to walk on eggshells around Ryan because she didn't want to be lectured. Ryan always felt as though he knew best about everything, which included the best places to vacation, politics, and wine. Molly didn't want an argument, so she dropped things quickly. By doing so, however, it also allowed Ryan to get away with his behavior.

Plenty of scenarios showed how Ryan was verbally abusive:

- He told her that she wasn't mature enough to have the same political views as him.
- He called her a klutz.

- She was identified as an amateur when she said that she didn't like red wine.
- He blamed her when his cases didn't turn out well.
- None of her furniture was good enough for his place.
- He told her that she'd regret breaking up with him.

There were times when he was verbally abusive that Molly called him out on it. That's when he would say, "I'm joking," as a way to help her forget about it. However, those kinds of tactics are common among bullies. They think that they can say whatever they want as long as they say that they're joking afterward. Joking or not, those kinds of comments hurt.

Molly's friends noticed that her behavior had changed in a negative way after dating Ryan. She was no longer as sure of herself as she used to be because Ryan made her question her value. Ryan made her feel as though her opinions didn't matter. That's why he booked Portland instead of Cape Cod. He ordered what he wanted her to have instead of asking her what she wanted. This was evident with the first date when he ordered a Cosmopolitan and again when he ordered the red wine.

Molly made a lot of excuses to explain the verbal abuse. She blamed it on him being stressed. The problem with this is that people who are stressed may be short but they should still be respectful. Ryan's comments were anything but respectful.

. . .

While Ryan loved Molly in his own way, it wasn't a balanced relationship. It was about control.

Healthy relationships are about compromise. There are times when there will be disagreements. However, it is the couple's ability to compromise that can be the make or break point. If one person is doing all of the compromising and the other person is getting their way all of the time, it throws the relationship off balance. At some point, the person who is always compromising loses who they are.

Molly took the time to reach out to her friends. She knew that she needed help to end things with Ryan. One helped her move her things out of his apartment when he was still at work. Then, they were at the bar, at a table behind her, when she met with Ryan to break things off. He yelled and created a scene. He threatened to 'make her pay' and told her that she was ruining his image and hers. That's when her friends chimed in. They told him to back off or they would be witnesses for getting Molly a restraining order against him.

Molly had a bit of explaining to do the next day when she told her law firm that she didn't want to be on any cases with Ryan, even though they were no longer dating. After explaining why, they understood and honored her wishes. She moved in with one of her friends until she was able to get a new apartment.

Molly had to start from scratch but it was worth it in the end. She knew that she didn't want to live in fear of the person she was dating. She also knew that she had to have her friends there as a support system.

Molly also attended some mental health counseling so that she could understand it wasn't her fault. Ryan had worn her down with his judging, criticizing, and undermining that she didn't know what her self-worth was anymore. Ryan was very good at accusing and blaming. After a few sessions with a counselor, she realized that she was a victim of verbal abuse and that he was responsible for what happened to him, not her.

Bullies typically don't change. They take on plenty of forms, too. They may be physically or verbally abusive. They may start out as the nicest guy around. In time, they'll show their true colors and manipulate situations so that they get their way.

When you're dating a bully, you have to know what to look for. Often it's your friends who will spot the differences in your behavior. Without the help of a support system, you could end up staying in a bad relationship for years. You make excuses for their behavior. You don't want to leave the relationship because you don't think that you can do any better. When your lives are intertwined, it's harder to take action, too, because you don't want to cause a huge disruption. In the end, bullies are always going to be bullies. Ending things with them will allow you to be more mentally stable and feel more confident in all aspects of your life.

VI

BREAKING UP IS HARD TO DO

Breaking up is often the easiest and healthiest way for you to move forward. If you don't break up, you're constantly going to have to face being in a relationship with someone who isn't right for you. Remember, dating is a tool used to help you determine if they're 'right' for you in terms of being a potential mate for life. If you find that a person is a narcissist, a freeloader, or a bully, they're not going to provide you with what you need in a healthy relationship.

Breaking up will allow you to take your life back. You will be able to learn from your past mistakes and make sure that you're free when the right person does come along.

Before you can actually say that you want to break up, you have to do some self-reflection. This often involves figuring out why the person is wrong for you and why it's time to end things.

12

WHY CERTAIN CHARACTERS DON'T MAKE GOOD PARTNERS

Molly had to learn the hard way that narcissists, freeloaders, and bullies don't make for good partners. However, because she dated them, she learned how to spot their behaviors. Dating allowed her to learn who she did and didn't want to be with. Each relationship taught her something else to look for so that she didn't settle for the wrong relationship.

THE PROBLEM WITH NARCISSISTS

Narcissists don't make good partners because they're too centered on themselves. Everything they do is to help themselves look good. It's hard to be in a relationship with a narcissist because you'll never come first. It's not always easy to realize that you're in a relationship with a narcissist, either. They may wine and dine you, but it's all in an effort to put the spotlight on themselves. They may make comments to their friends or co-workers like, "Look how well I treat my girlfriend."

. . .

With Molly and James, for example, James flew her to NYC and LA. He did this to make sure that he always had 'his biggest fan' around.

Staying with them means having to give up a piece of yourself. You have to decide whether this is something you really want. While narcissists are capable of love, it's a very different type of love. They'll never prioritize you because it's not in their nature. This means that you have to learn to live with being number two.

When you break up with a narcissist, they may not take well to the breakup because you are, essentially, saying that they aren't as important as they think they are. They also lose their top cheerleader. In the end, however, they'll do just fine because they have a large enough ego to handle it. They'll find someone else who will be their cheerleader because it's what they do.

With James, the breakup went relatively smoothly. He didn't fight it because he was focused on his image. He was confident that he'd have another girlfriend to replace Molly in no time.

THE PROBLEM WITH FREELOADERS

Freeloaders are those who don't know how to take care of themselves or feel as though someone else should be doing it for them. Some freeloaders continue to live with their parents well into their twenties without saving any money to move out. Other freeloaders jump from friend's couch to friend's couch. When you date a freeloader, you enable them.

By staying with someone like this, you continue to support them. While it's important to be a support to your partner, it shouldn't be one-sided. You shouldn't be responsible for financially supporting them, especially in the early stages of the relationship. If you or your partner choose to be a stay-at-home parent, for example, later on in the relationship, that's different. You're choosing for one person to support while the other person supports in a different way. There's still a balance of responsibility.

When you break up with a freeloader, they may become manipulative or pleading. While they may miss your company, their first thought is wondering how they're going to be supported. They don't want to lose their meal ticket. A clean break will allow you to walk away. It is not your responsibility to support anyone, so don't feel guilty about your actions.

Blake was manipulative. He needed Molly to support him, so he did what he could to stay. The only way that it worked was that Molly stayed strong to make sure that they separated.

THE PROBLEM WITH BULLIES

The problem with a bully is that they don't start out as a bully. They can be the nicest guy in the beginning, if not a bit over-confident. However, as they get more comfortable in the relationship, they begin to control you. They do this to give themselves more power.

The abuse isn't always physical. In fact, most of the time it isn't. They accuse and they blame. They disguise verbal abuse as jokes. They discount what you say. They undermine what you say, trivialize what you do and how you dress, and threaten when you do something of your own accord. In the end, you realize that you constantly live in fear of what your partner will say or do, and that's no way to live your life.

When you break up with a bully, they may threaten you because leaving means that they lose their power over you. They may get violent, plead, promise that they will change their ways, or manipulate you into staying. Due to the controlling nature of bullies, it's best to choose a location where you feel safe.

Ryan, for example, yelled. Luckily, Molly had chosen a public place for the breakup. Even then, Ryan got loud enough that the bartender had to remind him to lower his voice. Molly also told him that they could talk again in a few days, allowing for a 'cooling-off' period.

If you feel as though it could become violent, have friends around for moral support (and protection).

13

HOW TO KNOW WHEN IT'S TIME TO CALL IT QUITS

It's not always easy to know when to call it quits. Some relationships go on for years longer than they should because a person doesn't realize that they're with the wrong person, they make excuses for them, or they simply don't want to face single life again. As soon as you know that the person is wrong for you, it's time to end the relationship. Staying in a relationship that doesn't make you happy isn't going to help either one of you in the long run.

Everything may be going great for a long time. Then something changes. It is these changes that you have to look out for. It may be that a person feels that they have to control you since they can't control anything else in their life. They may realize that it's easier to sit back and let you support them instead of going back out to find a job. You have to be careful that you don't allow yourself to be a doormat in an effort to feel loved.

. . .

It's easy to make excuses for a partner. In some instances, you're justified in doing this. They have had a long day so they were a little grouchy. They received bad news earlier and they didn't want any more bad news coming from you. They wanted everything to go perfectly and were a little hypercritical of what you did or what you wore. These are okay in certain scenarios. However, if they become the norm, you have to realize this. You also have to realize that you deserve better.

We live in a society where people ask whether you're dating or married. Often, it's easier to be in a relationship because you have someone to lean on. You have someone who will be your 'plus-one' in various scenarios. You don't have to worry about showing up to social situations alone because you have your significant other to take with you.

Even if things aren't perfect, you make yourself believe that it's better to be in a relationship than to be single. Many people don't actually like to date. As a result, they find themselves partnering up and staying with someone out of obligation or because it feels comfortable.

You could go for years in this manner. Then you look at where you are. You're in a relationship with a person whom you don't see marrying and whom you could never imagine having kids with. Now what? You've wasted years in a relationship that you were simply too comfortable to get out of. You had a few happy moments with them, but you were never truly happy because they were wrong for you.

·   ·   ·

Calling it quits is hard because it requires you to step outside of your comfort zone. You may not want to do this for one reason or another. However, you have to muster up all of your energy to do it because it will make you happier in the end.

There are a few surefire ways to know that it's time to call it quits:

- All of your friends are pointing out flaws in the relationship.
- You don't feel like yourself when you're with him.
- You have had to give up things that you love.
- He's embarrassed you with his extreme behavior on more than one occasion.
- He takes advantage of your generosity.

There are plenty of other examples, too. In the end, you have to go with your gut. Have you ever thought to yourself, "What am I doing with him?" If you have, then you need to end things because you're only delaying the inevitable.

Remember that it's all about balance. If a person isn't balancing you out, they aren't a suitable partner for you. If you feel as though all of the attention is always on them or all of the responsibility is always on you, there's a problem with the balance. That's all the reason that you need to call it quits. If they can't even balance things out while you're dating, what hope do you have that it will improve when you're married?

. . .

It's best to think of dating as a trial period. At the end of the trial period, you can choose to say, "Yes, I want this," or, "No, I'd rather not." There's no right answer. Some people will say yes and some people will say no. It's your choice. If you don't like the person you're with when you're dating them, you're under no obligation to stay with them. You don't have to marry them. You can throw them back into the dating pool and move on. You can use these dating scenarios to learn from your past mistakes. This will make it easier to find what you are looking for.

You deserve to be happy. Calling it quits with a narcissist, a freeloader, or a bully will make you happy. It may not seem like it right away because you have left your comfort zone. You will find yourself in the dating pool, single and alone. It may not be easy. However, you won't be coupled with someone who doesn't value your opinions or picks on you for what you say or what you think. You can be free to be you without anyone judging you.

By freeing yourself of a partner who doesn't offer balance, you're able to move forward and date someone who can offer balance. When you finally find the right person, everything will fall into place. You can feel as though you're able to say or do anything without being judged. This is what you have to remember is waiting for you. As soon as you break up with the wrong person, you have the ability to find true love. This fact alone should motivate you.

. . .

It's not easy, but it's got to be done. Once you know that they're not right for you, it can be extremely freeing. You can release the burden that has been weighing on you so that you can start to feel like 'you' again.

14

TIPS TO MAKE A BREAKUP EASIER

Breaking up is hard to do. Some people are easier to break up with than others. What's important is that you stay strong and go forward with your plans. To avoid being talked back into a relationship, there are some tips to help you. This way, you can get out of the relationship as painlessly as possible.

Have a support system in place. This can be friends who will be there during the breakup or a close friend who you can move in with temporarily in order to remove yourself from the bad situation.

- Make a list of pros and cons of why you're in the relationship. The cons will outweigh the pros, which will serve as your reminder as to why things need to end.
- Break up with the person in a public place. You never know how a person is going to react when you choose to break up with them. By choosing a

public place, you have witnesses. It protects you in case the person gets loud or violent.

- Establish an exit strategy so that you can make the cleanest break possible. This is especially important if you live with the person or the two of you work together.
- Make it as quick as possible. There's no need to extend the breakup any longer than necessary. Let them know that things are over. You don't have to give any kind of reasoning as to why things are ending unless you choose to do so.

Think about how you want to be broken up with. There's no need to be mean or brutal about the way that you break up with someone. You loved them enough to be with them, so you should love them enough to end things in a civil way. Although they may not be right for you, it's still best to break up with them in a way that provides both of you with closure.

Closure is all about allowing both of you to have the tools to move on to healthy relationships later on. If you feel as though something was incomplete about a breakup or things didn't get said, it can cause hesitation when you want to move forward.

Choose a place for the breakup to happen. It's best to do it in a place that works for the two of you. If you're afraid of it being emotional, choose a place where the two of you can cry and hug it out. If you're afraid of it being violent, choose a public place. While you have to prioritize your safety, you also have to remember that breaking up with someone is a private ordeal. Don't invite them over to your place to break up with them as it won't allow you to escape when you're ready to leave.

Before you go into the setting where you're going to break up with the person, think about what you want. Remember that you're breaking up with them because you want a better life. Think about your opening line and how you're going to start off the conversation.

The conversation should be face-to-face. It's the decent thing to do. There's no need to ghost someone or send them a text. You wouldn't want to be broken up in that way, so don't be the person to do that.

Give both of you closure. Be direct without being mean. Explain that you want to break up. Provide a reason or two. If the person starts demanding answers, you can choose to tell them as much or as little as you want. In the end, you don't owe the person a play-by-play as to every reason why you want to break up. This is the case regardless of how long you have been with them.

If the two of you live together, have an exit strategy in place before you break up. This is often the reason why people stay in relationships longer than what is healthy. It's hard to come up with the finances to move out. It's also hard to take that step to divide everything. Ask a family member or a friend if you can stay with them for a few weeks until you get back on your feet. If you share finances, look at ways that you can focus on your financial freedom in the weeks leading up to your breakup.

In some instances, you have to take a week or two to create an exit strategy before you can break up with the person. Take this time so that it's easier to make it happen. However, don't focus so much on the exit that you let it consume you. If the exit strategy takes you a year, you're only delaying the inevitable. It will be more painful for both of you this way. Get out as quickly as possible, even if it means having to move back home temporarily.

If you work together, think about finding a new job. If you simply cannot find another job, talk to leadership. This will allow them to know about the issue so that they're aware if or when tensions rise.

Once you announce that you're breaking up with them, prepare for a lot of emotions. Even though you know that breaking up with them is the right thing to do, you're closing a chapter of your life. You may cry and feel as though you're making a mistake. You shared a part of your life with this person. It's understandable to feel sad. However, don't mistake the sadness for regret. You're breaking up with the person for a reason.

Let the other person get emotional, too. They may cry, demand answers from you, or shut down entirely. There may be no way of knowing how they're going to process the information. Allow them to grieve in their own way, even if it means leaving once you have shared what you want to share. Once they compose themselves, they may reach out to you to talk things out. In some instances, this 'talk' may happen several months after the breakup.

It all comes down to ending things in a way that works for both of you. Choose your words carefully so that you are direct and explanatory. Giving both of you the closure to move on is necessary. It will allow you to tie things up properly so that you don't feel as though you have the remnants of a past relationship hanging over you for months or even years following the breakup.

There's no need to rush into another relationship once you've ended this one, either. Use your time of being single as a way of healing. Do some self-reflection to figure out what went wrong, why it went wrong, and what you could have done differently. You may want to consider making an appointment with a relationship counselor, too. They can help you to grieve the loss of the relationship while also helping you to see that you did the right thing by exiting when you did.

VII

MOLLY'S HAPPILY EVER AFTER

Molly hasn't had an easy time when it comes to love. She's had to learn the hard way by dating a narcissist, a freeloader, and a bully. However, as each relationship ended, she learned more about herself and the world around her. The heartaches hurt, but she was able to move forward.

Now it's time for Molly to get her happily ever after by finding a positive relationship where her partner sees her as an equal as opposed to someone he can take advantage of in one way or another.

15

PROFILE: DEREK & MOLLY

Molly had to spend some time living the single life for a while. She had a few emotional ups and downs as a result of not wanting to get into another bad relationship. After spending about three months meeting with a relationship counselor, she had a better sense of who she was and what she wanted in a potential husband.

She had almost forgotten about the card that she had put in her pocket. The one that belonged to Derek. He had handed it to her in the courthouse one day. She couldn't figure out why she chose to keep it, but she did. She kept it on her dresser and finally picked it up. She fingered the edge of the card and made the decision to give him a call.

What should she say? She was never the direct kind of girl to take the initiative. Perhaps though she could be. She picked up her phone and dialed the number. It rang twice.

"Hello?"

"Hi, Derek?" Molly asked, not entirely sure it was him.

"This is he, who is calling?" he asked.

Molly laughed lightly, her nerves getting the best of her. "It's Molly. Um, we went to law school together and…"

"I know who you are, Molly," Derek chuckled. "How are you?"

"I'm good. I, well, I found your card that you gave me a few months ago," Molly said.

Derek smiled. "I was wondering if you were ever going to call. Would you like to grab drinks this evening and catch up?"

"I'd really like that."

"Great. Do you want to meet at Capitol Bar right across from the courthouse? Around six?" Derek asked.

"Sounds great. I'll see you, then," Molly said and she hung up the phone with a smile on her face.

The next day, Molly made sure that she looked extra good for court. A few of her friends commented, asking what the occasion was. Molly put up her hand and just said that she was meeting a friend for drinks. When they pressed for details, she told them that it was nothing. While she had always liked Derek in school, she didn't know much about him. She wasn't ready to jump into anything serious. If there was one thing she had learned from her past relationships it was that she needed to be a bit more guarded with her heart.

The day flew by, and before she knew it, she was walking across the street to go to Capitol Bar. Derek was standing at the entrance.

"You look great," he smiled and held the door open for her.

"Thank you," she said.

"So, am I to assume you're not with that prosecutor anymore?" Derek asked once they were settled at the bar.

She shook her head. "No. That ended months ago."

"I'm glad to hear it. He was always a bit of an egomaniac in the courtroom, so I can't imagine what you went through." Derek noticed Molly shift on her bar stool, obviously uncomfortable with the topic. "Anyways, how have you been? You're in with a really good firm."

Molly smiled. "I have been really good. I took a cruise last year with my girlfriends. It was so much fun that I want to go again. I just need to find time in this crazy busy schedule."

Derek nodded. "I understand that completely. I haven't had a chance to go on a vacation in a while. I'm enjoying the work that I do, though."

"Me, too. It's nice to help others. The courtroom can be a little intimidating sometimes, though," Molly admitted.

"I hear that. Listen, why don't we grab a table in the dining room? It won't be as loud and we can get a bite to eat, too. We can continue our conversations with a little more privacy," Derek suggested.

"Lead the way," Molly said, picking up her glass.

Everything about the date went naturally. The conversation flowed, with each of them having the opportunity to share about what was happening at work and personally. When the check came, Molly found herself holding her breath for a moment.

Derek took care of the check and chuckled. "Why do you look relieved?"

Molly started laughing. "I, umm, I dated a guy who forgot his wallet on our first date."

"Oh, no he didn't," Derek said, shocked.

Molly nodded her head. "Yeah, that pretty much set the tone for the rest of the relationship."

Derek shook his head. "Well, that's not something you'll have to worry about with me. I'm perfectly capable of picking up the check when we go out. Speaking of which," he smiled, "would you like to go out this weekend? My sister is in a play at the local theater. I promised I'd go and support her on opening night."

"Really? Absolutely. I'd love to go," Molly said.

The rest of the week went well at work. Molly spent almost an hour on the phone with Derek every night. They would sit up while watching a show at their apartments while talking about what was going on. It was a fun date night while getting to enjoy their privacy at the same time.

By the time Saturday came, Molly was beyond excited to see Derek again. He was coming by around four to pick her up. The show was at five, and he told her that he had dinner reservations at eight.

Molly had on a flowery spring dress and was just strapping on her sandals when the doorbell rang.

"Hi, gorgeous," Derek smiled and gave Molly a kiss on the cheek.

She couldn't help but blush. "Hey."

Derek held open the door to the apartment. She locked the door and they took the stairs together. Then he held the door to his convertible open and made sure she was in and comfortable before closing it. "You ready?" he asked.

Molly nodded. "Ready."

As Derek drove to the theater, he talked. "Now, I can't promise how good this show is going to be. It's actually a montage of different Shakespeare plays. It's a community theater project my sister Claire has been involved in for a few years now. She loves it, so I'm always in favor of supporting her."

Molly laughed. "I'm sure it will be great. I love Shakespeare. It's also really great that you're so supportive of your sister. Do you have other siblings?"

"No, she's it. She's three years younger than I am, so I grew up being very protective of her. Family is important to me," he explained.

Molly frowned. "I'm not very close with my parents. They always seem to be busy with other things. They divorced when I was ten. One lives on one side of the country and the other lives on the other side."

"So, you chose to live right in the middle?" Derek chuckled.

Molly laughed. "Yeah. It was easier than choosing a side. Literally."

Derek pulled into a parking spot and ran around to open Molly's door. The fact that he was being so chivalrous was not lost on her. She thanked him again.

As they walked into the theater, Derek weaved his fingers into hers. He gave a little squeeze as soon as he saw his sister running at them.

"You're here. And you must be Molly!" Claire smiled and came in for a hug from both Derek and Molly.

Molly hugged her back. "Nice to meet you. I'm excited to see the show. Derek says that you're a great actress."

"I doubt he said that, but you're sweet. I gotta get back, so I'll catch you guys after the show," Claire said and jogged back to the side entrance.

"She is the outgoing one in the family," Derek laughed and he guided Molly to their seats.

The play was great. Molly couldn't help but smile at the way that Derek clapped furiously after each one of his sister's performances. She was really talented, too. Spending the evening there was more fun than Molly had had in a long time. Knowing that Derek's arm was wrapped around her shoulder most of the night was nice, too.

Afterward, Derek dropped a bouquet of flowers off to his sister. Then he and Molly were off to a restaurant for dinner.

"So, I wanted to ask you something," Molly said, taking a sip of her drink at the table.

Derek smiled. "Okay."

"Well, now that I met your sister, I wanted to ask what you meant that day I saw you in the courthouse. You know, when you told me that your sister had dated a guy like that," Molly said.

Derek shifted in his booth. "Yeah, I forgot I told you that. It's just that she dated a really controlling guy for almost two years. He was emotionally abusive toward her. Toward the end, it got physical, too."

"She's out of the relationship now, though?" Molly asked.

Derek nodded. "Yeah. I helped her get out of it. Now I am always on the lookout to make sure that friends don't fall into that kind of situation. When I saw how easy it was for my sister, I knew you probably didn't realize what you were in for."

Molly nodded but didn't say anything right away. "It took a while. I was already starting to have my doubts before you said anything. Your words definitely hit deep, though."

"Well, it all worked out in the end. After all, I'm sitting across from you and he's not," Derek said with a wink.

Molly smiled. "And I'm so glad that you are."

"Don't worry. I've had my fair share of bad relationships, too," Derek said.

"Oh?" Molly was interested but didn't want to pry if he didn't want to divulge that information just yet.

Derek nodded. "After a year of dating a woman, I was ghosted. She moved across the country and figured it was easier to ghost me than to actually have a conversation. Then there was the woman who wanted me to buy her everything and take her everywhere. I think she was just using me for my money when she found out I was a lawyer."

Molly smiled. "Freeloader? Very familiar with that one."

Derek laughed. "Yeah, dating isn't always the easiest thing to do."

They both agreed. After that dinner, it was very easy for Derek and Molly to be in each other's company. They had a lot in common and the conversations always flowed between them. There was never any awkward silence.

· · ·

Before Molly knew it, the firm was dropping off a holiday party invitation on her desk. She felt a lump in her throat because last year she went with Ryan. However, she knew that Derek was very different. She called to ask him to her party. He agreed under the condition that she'd go to his, which was the very next night.

Molly couldn't help but smile as she put on her red dress and silver shoes. Derek would be picking her up for the holiday party in no time. There was a knock at the door and he was standing there in a suit with a festive red vest.

"You look great," she smiled.

"So do you," Derek said.

As the two of them drove to the holiday party, Derek talked. "Is there anything I need to know about your firm?"

"What do you mean?" Molly asked.

"Every firm has its quirks. You've been there for over a year now, so I just like to know what I'm walking into," Derek said.

Molly nodded, understanding what he was talking about. "The firm likes to see who people show up with. It helps them to decide who is grounded enough to become partner."

"And you would like to make partner, right?" Derek asked.

"Of course. Don't you?" Molly asked.

Derek nodded. "Of course. I think that we make a great couple, so it shouldn't be any issue."

Molly frowned. "One other thing. Last year, I took the prosecutor."

Derek nodded again. "I figured as much. Everyone will just have to see that you have moved on." He gave her knee a light squeeze as they pulled up to the country club where the party was being held. She was happy that Derek understood that she didn't have the easiest past.

"You brought the enemy?" Molly's boss approached her and Derek as they came in.

Derek laughed. "Pleasure to actually meet you, sir."

Molly's boss shook his hand. "This guy is good. If he's your date, keep a close eye on him. We've been trying to get him to our firm for a while now."

Molly's eyebrows darted up. "Oh, really?"

Derek shook his head. "He's being way too kind. They offered me a job once over a year ago."

"And you turned it down," Molly's boss said.

Derek blushed. "That's because I know that you don't allow employees to date one another. And I've had my eye on this girl for quite some time."

Molly's cheeks turned red. "You never told me that."

Molly's boss chuckled. "Well, you picked a good one. Merry Christmas," he said and gave Derek a heavy pat on the shoulder as he walked off to greet more people coming in.

Molly couldn't stop smiling at Derek. He hadn't told her that he had been interested in her for over a year. She wondered if it had started back in college. She wanted to ask but didn't want to make a big deal about it. Derek reached for her hand and guided her to the dance floor where a few other couples were gliding across it.

"I guess my secret's out," he whispered to her.

Molly nodded. "It sure is."

"I've had a crush on you since law school. I just never had the courage to say anything. Then every time I wanted to make my move, I heard that you were involved with someone," Derek explained.

. . .

Molly went to say something but Derek interrupted her.

"I'm not complaining. I figure that it was all meant to be the way that it turned out. After all, you're in my arms and dancing with me now, right?"

"Right," Molly smiled and kissed him on the dance floor.

The next day, it was time to do it all over again, only it was at Derek's law firm. They had their party on the penthouse floor of the building they were in.

Derek made his rounds, introducing Molly to everyone he worked with. She shook hands and smiled. A few people already knew who she was just because of being in the courthouse at the same time.

When they were on the dance floor, Derek leaned in close. "I'm falling in love with you, Molly."

Molly froze. Love? That was such a big word. They'd already been dating a few months, but those words scared her. "Thank you," she said with a smile.

He kissed her cheek. "You're welcome. I don't want you to feel pressured to say it back." He meant those words, too. He was willing to take it slow with her because he knew that she had dealt with more heartache than any girl should have to deal with.

It took Molly a full extra month to be able to say the words back to Derek.

After she took him to the restaurant where she goes at least one Friday out of every month to meet her friends, she said it in the car ride back to her apartment. "I love you," she said to him as they sat at a red light.

He turned to her. "Really?"

"Really."

"Good," he smiled, "because I love you, too."

It seemed as though that helped everything click together for them in every way possible. The very next week, Molly had amazing news that she wanted to share with Derek. "I want to see you tonight. I don't want to tell you my news over the phone," she told him.

"Can I come over? I'll bring dinner from your favorite Chinese restaurant," Derek offered.

When he knocked with the food in one hand, Molly blurted out her news. "I made partner!" She was practically dancing around with the news finally out.

"Honey, that's amazing! I'm so proud of you!" Derek put down the food, picked her up and spun her around, closing the door to her apartment in the process.

"I was a little nervous to tell you because you haven't made partner at your firm yet," Molly admitted.

"Don't be ridiculous. I want you to share everything with me. I'll get there. If I'm not mistaken, you were better in some of the law classes we took, too. I'm sure you're just a little better than me in the courtroom, too," he winked.

Molly smiled. "You're too kind."

"Nonsense. You're the best lawyer there is. Now, come on, let's dig in," he said, ripping open the white cartons on the counter.

. . .

The next few months were very busy for Molly as her case-load increased with being a partner. Derek helped her, stopping in with Chinese food and pizza when he could. He also stopped by to ask her something important.

"Hey," he said over dinner one night, "I know you said you haven't been really close with your parents since they divorced."

"Yeah," she said, wondering what he was getting at.

"Well, I was just wondering if maybe you wanted to take a visit with me to each coast. I have a ton of miles that I've got sitting in my frequent flyer account. Plus I know you're coming up on some downtime," he said.

Molly thought about it for a moment. It had been almost a year since she'd seen her dad. She had seen her mom around Thanksgiving, but that was nearly four months ago. "Okay, that sounds like fun. Oregon and Virginia, here we come!"

"Great," Derek smiled. "I'll take care of all of the flights."

Virginia was first on the list. She was happy to get to see her mother. She was an only child, so they shared a bond. The only problem was that her mother's husband was very possessive of her time. Molly always felt as though she was a bother. When she told her mother about it one time, her mother said that she was being ridiculous.

Molly's stepfather was the one who picked the two of them up at the airport. "I'm so surprised that he's making the effort to pick us up," Molly said as she wheeled her baggage out to the curb to meet him.

Derek shrugged. "Maybe he's decided to be more involved."

"Maybe," Molly said.

The drive to the house was pretty quiet. Howard, Molly's stepfather, talked about all of the new construction going on. He and Molly's mom had recently retired, so they were focusing on finding some new hobbies in the area.

"Do you both drink wine?" he asked.

Molly and Derek both nodded.

"Great. We'll head to a few wineries this weekend. It will be a lot of fun," Howard said.

Molly smiled. Everything was going really well.

Molly's mom was home when they got there. She came out and gave Derek a big hug. "I've heard so many good things about you!"

"Me, too, ma'am. You've raised an amazing daughter," Derek said.

"Oh, you're just as sweet as Molly told me you are," her mom teased.

Once Derek and Molly got into the guest room, Derek closed the door. "I thought you said that you weren't close with your parents?"

Molly shrugged. "Maybe retirement has changed them. I'm really glad, though. I love my mom a lot. Howard seems really different, too."

. . .

The rest of the weekend went really well. Everyone's conversations flowed, especially at the wineries. Howard seemed genuinely interested in what Molly was doing. He even talked in detail with Derek over dinner. Molly wondered if it made a difference now that she was out of the house. Now that he had Mom all to himself all the time, it was enough to calm him down. Molly didn't know what it was, but she couldn't have been more thrilled with how the weekend went.

After another crazy week at work, Derek and Molly were off to Oregon for a long weekend with her dad. He had never remarried, so it was just him in a giant house near Mount Hood.

"Dad!" Molly greeted her dad, who was standing at the bottom of the escalator when she and Derek were headed to baggage claim.

"Hey, sweetie. I'm so glad that you decided to come for a visit. And that you brought a man with you," he said, smiling at Derek.

"Very nice to meet you, sir," Derek said, shaking his hand.

"Nonsense, call me Bill. Let's get your luggage and head back to the house, huh?" Bill said.

Molly nodded, holding hands with Derek. "He's really outgoing. I see where you get it from," Derek whispered.

Molly smiled. She had always been close to her dad. It was nice to see that he was doing well and happy.

She hadn't been out to his new house, so it was a surprise when they all pulled up into the driveway. It was considerably bigger than Molly had expected. "Wow, Dad, it's huge."

"Well, I like to have my space," Bill explained.

Molly explained that for Derek. "My dad really likes his music. My guess is he's got a recording studio in one of these rooms."

Her dad started chuckling. "You know me too well."

The weekend was spent hiking in the mountains, visiting breweries, and enjoying conversations in the living room. Molly noticed that there were a few times where her dad had Derek in a room, talking to him. When she pressed Derek for details, he said that there was nothing to be concerned about.

On the flight home, Molly leaned back. "I'm so happy right now. Visiting both of my parents was refreshing. It was nice to spend some time with them. You're the first person I've ever taken home to meet my parents, too," she admitted.

Derek smiled. "Well, that means a lot to me."

Molly caught him winking at the flight attendant, who, in turn, nodded. She was going to ask what that was about when Derek stood up and reached into his pocket. He leaned forward into her seat and held out a box.

"Would you marry me, Molly?"

Just then, the pilot came on the overhead. "Folks, there's been a proposal in the sky. The man in seat 22B just proposed to the woman in seat 22A."

A number of people leaned forward to see who the pilot was talking about.

Molly turned bright red. She was breathless.

"I couldn't wait any longer. I want to spend the rest of my life with you," Derek said. "What do you say?"

Molly nodded. "I say yes. Of course, I say yes."

. . .

Derek slipped the ring on her finger and gave her a kiss. Then the flight attendant walked over with two flutes of champagne. "Congratulations!" she said and the passengers and crew began clapping.

"I had no idea that this was going to happen," Molly said, clinking her glass with Derek's.

"I know. I was going to wait for a nice, quiet dinner, but I wanted to make a show of it. I'm sorry if I embarrassed you, but your dad gave me his permission and I couldn't wait," Derek said.

"It's perfect," Molly said, staring down at her white diamond ring for a moment.

By the time the plane landed, Molly and Derek realized they didn't want to stay engaged long. They wanted to get married as soon as possible. It was already March, so they decided that a fall wedding would be perfect. It gave them seven months to get the planning done. She was on the phone with her parents while sending texts to her friends on the drive home. It was all so exciting.

Wedding planning wasn't as stressful as Molly would have expected. Both of her parents chipped in for the wedding, allowing for a wedding planner who took care of almost everything.

Molly and Derek had dinner with his parents and sister one night, giving Molly a chance to get to know everyone a bit more. They were just as kind as Derek had described. Her sister smiled and told Molly she knew it would happen from that second date at the theater.

"I was hoping that you'd be willing to do something with me," Molly approached Derek one night as they sat across from each other at a restaurant.

"Anything," Derek smiled.

"I'd like to sign up for a six-week premarital counseling program," Molly said.

Derek hesitated. "Do you think we really need that?"

"No, not necessarily. But I'd like to make sure that we're on the same page for everything," she explained.

Derek nodded. "If it's important to you, we will absolutely do it."

"Thank you," she smiled. This helped her to breathe easier, knowing that there was no way that she could possibly make a mistake at this point. He was truly the right man for her.

Everything Molly had ever hoped for was finally coming true.

When October 12 showed up and she slipped into her wedding dress, she knew that Derek was her forever. Claire, Derek's sister, was her maid of honor. Then she had three of her closest friends as bridesmaids, including Megan. Derek asked Molly's stepfather to be one of his groomsmen so that he would have a role within the wedding since her dad was the one giving her away. Her stepfather was honored to have the position.

Molly and Derek were thrilled to have both families so heavily involved in the wedding.

Standing in front of each other in the church, staring into

each other's eyes, everything felt right. As the priest spoke, Molly got goosebumps. This was really happening. She was getting married to the man of her dreams.

"I do." They were the easiest words Molly had ever spoken.

After the wedding, Molly and Derek took two weeks off to go on an amazing cruise. When they got back, they spent nearly a week moving everything into a new house that they had bought.

A year later, Molly announced that she was pregnant. Happy endings do happen, and Molly and Derek were thrilled to be able to tell the story of theirs to anyone who would listen.

16

RELATIONSHIP COMMENTARY

There's clearly a big difference between Derek and all of the other men whom Molly had dated. One of the most obvious is that there's a balance within the relationship. He doesn't take her for granted at any point of their dating. He is respectful, understands the balance of power and money, and treats her fairly in front of friends, family members, co-workers, and when they're all alone.

Molly has learned a few things along the way, too. She understands more about what to look for in a partner. She knows that she doesn't have to settle. She is also okay with talking about her past, knowing that it helped shape her. Had she kept all of her past relationships a secret, it would have created a barrier between her and Derek. She knew that to have a healthy relationship with him, he needed to know why some of her past relationships didn't end well. He shared about his past, too. It was something that they were able to laugh at because they had left those relationships where they belong: in the past.

. . .

There are a few signs that Derek is the real deal. He's not hiding anything and Molly feels more comfortable opening up her heart:

- He's respectful of her.
- He's close with his family.
- He shares about past relationships.
- He doesn't push her past her limits.
- They talk openly about anything and everything.

Everything about Derek and Molly is balanced. He introduces her to his friends and she introduces him to hers. They're not trying to hide anything from one another. They're also eager and excited to meet people from each other's lives instead of trying to avoid those aspects.

Derek knew enough about Molly's past to make sure to tread lightly, especially when it came to saying, "I love you." This can be the make or break point in many relationships. It may be said too fast before the feelings are actually there. It may also be said back to make sure that the person doesn't feel bad for saying it even when it's not reciprocated.

Derek accepted the fact that Molly needed time. However, that didn't stop him from saying the words to her. He spoke his feelings and didn't expect anything in return. When she finally did return the feelings with her words, he repeated that he loved her, confirming that his feelings for her hadn't changed.

Strong relationships are about balance, communication, and compromise. Molly and Derek were capable of achieving all of these things together. They balanced each other out at work, always respecting that they were busy. They figured out how to make things work, even if it meant talking over the phone while watching TV instead of physically being near each other.

There was also a lot of communication. Derek opened up to Molly and Molly did the same with Derek. There was no topic that was off limits because that's what makes a healthy relationship. If one was constantly hiding secrets or not sharing enough of themselves, it would cause hurdles in the relationship.

Furthermore, there was a lot of compromise. They learned how to lift each other up. At no point did Derek feel threatened when Molly made partner before him. Instead, he was thrilled for her. It's the way that a partner should be. If he's not supportive, he's not truly focused on what's best for her.

In the end, Molly felt comfortable with committing to Derek because there were no red flags. Her friends loved him, her co-workers loved him, and her parents loved him. He took the time to make sure that she could see her parents. He also asked for her father's permission before proposing to her. It showed that he had a lot of respect for Molly and wanted to make sure it was perfect. They also went to premarital counseling. While it's not something Derek thought they necessarily needed, it was important to Molly. As such, it became important to Derek. He knew that she would feel more confident saying, "I do," if they went through the counseling program.

Finding the right partner is not always easy. Although some people make it look so, most people have to learn the hard way, like Molly. When you are in a relationship, you have to give it a hundred percent. If you see red flags or lose your desire to be in the relationship, end things. It will allow you to move on so that you can get into a relationship that does hold promise for a future.

VIII

MOVING ON & MOVING UP

Knowing that you're in a bad relationship is the start of your new life. Once you're aware that there's a problem, it provides you with a light at the end of the tunnel. You can start to make steps toward getting out of the bad relationship. You can take the time to heal mentally and emotionally before you move on to another relationship.

Moving on from a relationship, whether it lasted a week or a year, can be hard. You're suddenly alone. No matter how wrong they were for you, you may have loved them or at least, loved your time with them. There's no specific amount of time to heal. Some people may need more or less time to recover.

What's important is that you don't rush into anything until you're truly ready. Otherwise, you're likely to jump into another bad relationship because you're desperate to not be alone.

Now that you've figured out some tips to find out what makes a relationship bad, you can get out of them and avoid them in the future. You can move out of a bad relationship and move on with your life.

Moving on and moving up into a better relationship can take just as many skills as it takes to get out of a bad relationship. After all, the goal is to learn from your mistakes. This takes a bit of self-reflection. However, anything worth doing is worth doing right. You owe this to yourself. Your happiness depends on it.

17

HOW TO GET OVER HIM

How do you truly get over someone? When you start to date someone, you open your heart and you let them in. They start to learn about who you are and what makes you tick. You start to learn about them, too. Your lives start to intertwine. You may even choose to become intimate with that person.

Walking away from the relationship, no matter how toxic, can be difficult. You have already walked away. Now you have to learn to look forward instead of looking behind you. If you want to give any future relationship a chance, you have to be truly over your last one. Otherwise, you will hold on to too much resentment. The new partner won't stand a chance because your head won't be fully in the game.

Take the time to heal. This could be days, weeks, or even months. If it's taking you years to get over someone, whether they were simply a partner or a spouse, it may be time to make an appointment with a counselor. While there is no specific time to heal, you don't want to allow a bad relationship to take more of your life than it already has.

Self-care is important at all times but more so after a breakup. You need to focus on you and no one else. Don't let anyone try to take your 'me' time away from you. There are plenty of things that you can do:

- Visit a spa for the day.
- Go for a hike.
- Spend some time visiting family or friends out of town.
- Binge-watch some of your favorite movies on the couch.

Go ahead and give yourself the time to mourn the loss of the relationship. After that, you can start to move forward a bit.

There needs to be some time for self-reflection, too. It's different for everyone. You may not feel as though you're a whole person now that you are without your partner. However, it's what's best for you. The sooner you come to terms with this, the easier it will be to move forward.

You have to remind yourself why you left the relationship to begin with. They were controlling. They were focused on themselves. They were using you. Whatever the reason was, you chose to leave the relationship. You gathered enough strength to walk yourself out of a relationship that wasn't healthy.

While it may not seem like it now that you're alone, you did the right thing. Being able to move past the relationship may take a while. What's critical is that you see the bad relationship for what it was. It was a stepping stone. You needed to be with that person in order to learn what you don't want. You are not responsible for how they feel or what they do next. Your first priority has to be you.

One of the most important things to remember is that you're worthy of love. You deserve all of the happiness in the world. When you're out of a relationship that wasn't positive, it can take a toll on your self-esteem. This means that you have to work to make sure that you take the time to build yourself back up.

What are you really good at? Sometimes, it's about focusing on what makes you unique. Maybe you have a great career or you're a great friend. Maybe you have some really great talents that you can explore. Whatever it is, it's what makes you who you are.

Now that you're not in a relationship, it may be time to get your life back on track. The relationship that you were in wasn't evenly balanced, which means that you likely had to give up some of who you were in order to make things work. It's time to reclaim that. It may mean pursuing your career, going back to school, reconnecting with your friends, or even testing out a new hobby.

When your self-esteem has really taken a beating, you may not feel worthy. Your self-worth is of the utmost importance. You have to do whatever it takes to build that up. It might take some time. Your friends may need to help you. A mental health counselor may need to help you. Often, however, it is all about learning to love yourself.

There's no way that you can love someone else, or allow yourself to be loved, until you truly love yourself. This isn't just about being comfortable with your looks. It's about being comfortable with the thoughts in your head. You can't let someone else dictate how you feel about yourself. If there was someone in your life telling you that you weren't important or that you weren't special, you need to remind yourself that it was for purposes of control. They had to tell you those things so that they could control you.

Mantras can be extremely powerful. The repetitive nature of a mantra can bury deep into your subconscious so that you begin to believe the words. A mantra can be anything you want it to be.

- I am worthy of love.
- I am a strong individual.
- I love who I am.
- No man can control me.

You can decide on the words. Once you choose what your mantra is going to be, remember it. Recite it. Write it down. Keep the words in a place where you can see them often. A note taped to your vanity mirror at home can be a daily reminder when you're getting ready every morning. A Post-it note on your computer with the mantra can help to keep you focused at work. When you feel your self-esteem plummeting, recite the mantra.

Don't just say the mantra in your head, either. Saying it out loud can help it to reverberate. By speaking it out loud, you hear it with your own words, hearing it as truth. This can be the powerful tool that you need to overcome the harm that a past relationship has done to you.

You have to find a way to love yourself. When you can love yourself, it allows you to love others. It also allows you to let others in to love you.

When you start to love yourself, it will be easier to see why the relationship was bad. You deserved so much more than what he could offer you. You may need to remind yourself of this periodically, especially if you have the sudden urge to call him and ask to get back together. You do not want to take this backward step.

Stay strong and put the relationship behind you. When you can look forward, it will be better for you. The future holds all sorts of promises as long as you're not looking at it with blinders on.

18

WHERE TO FIND GOOD DATES

I t may not seem like it now, but you're going to date again. It might not be today and it might not be tomorrow. However, there will come a point where you feel comfortable with yourself again. This is when you'll want to get back out there and find someone who can be your forever.

You may want to consider where the best (and worst) places are to find dates. Much of this will depend on what your goals are. Do you want to find someone to fill a void or do you want to find a suitable partner? There's a big difference in where you'll go depending on what your answer is. Your goal should always be to focus on someone who is a suitable partner. If you're looking to fill a void, you probably need to spend a bit more time in self-reflection.

The good news is that you won't be alone forever. You are in control of whether you're alone or if you find a partner. You might need to take the first step, though. Once you're ready, you simply have to put yourself out there. When you're open to the possibility of dating and finding a partner, it will happen.

There are plenty of places to find good dates. However, there's no surefire way to avoid finding a few duds no matter how you find someone. It's important to know what you're looking for in a partner before you even enter the dating scene. This will make it easier for you to stay away from the ones who will only cause you heartache later on.

SHARED HOBBIES

Think about the different things that you enjoy doing. When you can meet someone doing something that you love, it instantly gives the two of you some common ground to share. It can make it easier to connect right away as opposed to searching for something to talk about. There's nothing worse than an awkward silence when you meet someone for the first time. Having the ability to get dialogue started will make it easier to move on to all sorts of other topics.

You may want to go to the gym, get involved with a sport, or even take a wine-tasting class or a DIY class. Whatever it is, you can go in with an open mind. If you meet someone, great. If not, continue it because you love it, not because you were hoping to meet someone.

ONLINE DATING

There are a ton of websites out there that will play match-maker for you. While these can be great, you also have to avoid being catfished. Make sure that you're able to see a photo of the person. Ask to have a video date where you can see who he is live before meeting him in person. Don't be afraid to talk for a week or two online before agreeing to meet. If things don't add up, such as him never being able to video chat or not being able to talk on the phone at certain times of the day, question it. If you're still not getting the right vibes, remember that you can walk away.

In order to be successful with online dating, you need to be honest about the entire process. Build your profile with a photo of how you look on a daily basis. Be brutal about what you want in a partner. While it may not provide you with as many matches, that's okay. It's better to weed out all of the unsuitable partners as early on as possible. This way, you don't waste your time and you're not putting your heart in harm's way, either.

When you're more honest, you're likely to get matched with people who are also being honest. The brutal honesty of your answers will scare away those who just want to play games.

FRIENDS

Your friends may want to play matchmaker because they want to see you happy. Before you let them set you up with just anyone, make sure you find out how well they know the person. Ask a few questions about who the person is and what they know about how the person is in different situations.

If you choose not to go out with the person or you do and don't like where it's headed, end things. Just because a friend set you up doesn't mean that you have to stay with the person.

Your friends may be trying to do what's right for you, but only you are the one capable of knowing that. Have some fun and try a date or two. If it doesn't work out, don't hesitate to end things. If your friends are truly looking out for you, they will respect your decisions.

SPONTANEITY

The reality is that you can meet someone anytime, anywhere. Maybe your hat blows off on the beach and the person who catches it will be your soulmate. Maybe you're in the grocery store and you reach for the same head of lettuce that someone else does. You cannot control whom you meet on a day-to-day basis. If you meet someone in your daily routine, take a chance to see where it leads.

It comes down to being open to the various opportunities that take place each and every day. If someone asks you out and you think that you might like them, go ahead and say, "Yes." There's nothing stopping you. You're an adult and therefore, you have the ability to date someone if they ask. Don't be so closed off that people are scared to approach you. Furthermore, don't turn away a potential future with someone just because it happened in a way that you weren't expecting. You can't force the way that you are going to meet someone just like you can't force the chemistry (or lack thereof) with someone.

Remember too, that you don't have to be the one to sit back and wait for them to ask you out. You can be the person to make the first move. While this may be completely out of your comfort zone, it may be what you need. Consider the ways that you can break the cycle of what's happened in the past. If all of your past relationships (which have failed) started because they pursued you, turn the tables.

There's nothing wrong with being the pursuer. It shows that you're calm, collected, and confident. When you're able to approach someone that you like and ask them out on a date, it can prove to them and to you that you're in control. It shows that you have a high level of self-esteem and that you do in fact love yourself.

What's important to remember is that there is no 'perfect' place to find a good date. What worked for someone you know may not work for you. Be open every day to the idea of finding love. It may find you when you least expect it.

19

HOW TO WEED OUT THE BAD SEEDS

Before you feel comfortable about weeding out the bad seeds, you have to realize that you're not obligated to date anyone. If someone asks you out, you can say no. If someone wants to play matchmaker, you can say no. You are in charge of who you go out with. You're also not obligated to give someone a reason why. "No, thank you." That's all you need to say if someone asks you on a date and you're not interested.

Moving forward with this knowledge can help you to focus on being in happier, healthier relationships. It empowers you to stay out of bad relationships because of obligation, guilt, or any other false feelings that you may have.

It's not always easy to see the undesirable qualities in a person when you start dating someone, especially if you find them attractive or funny. Often we try to see the good in people and make excuses for anything that we don't like.

However, that can lead to weeks, months, or even years with the wrong partner.

Listen to the red flags that pop up periodically in conversations. Does he have to have the last word? Does he try to dictate what you buy or what you eat? Does he ask about how you're doing? Does he share intimate information about himself? Ask some of these questions while you're out on a date. If you don't like the answers to the questions, it might be that the person is a bad seed.

Molly learned how to weed out the bad seeds. She went out with friends and talked to guys at clubs and at bars. She would shake her head or use body language to show that she wasn't interested. After a while, one of her friends asked, "What gives?"

Molly shrugged. "I know what I'm looking for."

Her friends teased her and told her that she was being too picky. She countered by telling them that they weren't being picky enough.

This was something that Molly had learned from going to some counseling sessions. Although dating is fun, it doesn't have to be a priority. She was allowed to be single without feeling pressured to be in a relationship.

. . .

When you're more comfortable with being alone too, it doesn't feel as though you have to rush into a relationship. If you constantly fear being alone, you'll rush into any relationship that presents itself. However, some of these relationships may be bad for you. Rather than investing more time of your life into a bad relationship, learn how to be alone. Enjoy being alone.

When you're ready to move on to a relationship, you can do so with more confidence, knowing that you can weed out a bad seed periodically when you come across one.

20

FALLING IN LOVE WITHOUT PAST MISTAKES HAUNTING YOU

F alling in love is exciting. When you feel that true connection with someone, you want to open up your heart and let them in. It's not always that easy. As a result of past mistakes, you may have built a wall up around your heart. It may be hard to let someone get close or you may struggle with saying, "I love you."

After all, you felt those feelings before. Or at least you thought you did. How do you know that this relationship is any different?

Unfortunately, you don't know. However, it's important that you take the risk. Love is worth it.

There's always that 'gut' feeling. It's worth listening to, at least in the beginning. If your gut tells you that they're not a forever thing, then there's likely a reason for you feeling that way. Don't try to force a relationship into working. It either works or it doesn't.

You cannot hold your current partner accountable for all of your past partners' mistakes. To do so would be unfair to him as well as to you. Your new partner is a clean slate. They weren't the one to judge you, talk down to you, or take advantage of you. To assume that they will do so will make it harder for them to get to know the real you.

Let the person you're dating in. Let them see who the real you is. Dating isn't just for your benefit. It's for their benefit, too. They may have a list of credentials that they're looking for in a potential forever, too. A relationship can be ended by either party.

If you don't let the person in to see the real you, you're just as guilty as some of your past relationships. You're putting on a facade where the person doesn't know who you are. Instead, you're only providing a surface level glimpse of who you really are.

Until you let the past mistakes stop haunting you, it may be difficult to get into any kind of long-term relationship. The other person will see that you're holding back on one level or another. While they may try to push past your walls, they may eventually decide that you're not ready. Rather than investing any more time in a 'work in progress', they may decide that it's best to move on.

.   .   .

This can be hard. You don't want to get into a relationship where someone is giving you an ultimatum. You can't simply 'get past' a relationship because your current partner told you that you need to do so. This is why it's best not to get involved in the dating scene until you're truly past the relationship. Otherwise, you're wasting time and hurting feelings.

Depending on the situation of your past relationships, it might be necessary to sit down with a relationship counselor. Don't assume that relationship counselors are solely for couples. You can go to a counselor as a way to figure out how to get your head back in the game. They can talk to you about what went wrong in past relationships. They can help you to figure out that it wasn't your fault that things went south. They can also help you to see why you were pulled into a relationship so deep so that you can spot issues faster next time.

Remember, dating is all about learning what you do and don't like. It allows you to learn from your mistakes. If you don't like a certain personality type, no one is going to fault you for that. Instead, take pride in the fact that you figured it out so that you can move forward into a relationship with a person who has a personality that you do like.

When you have moved past your bad relationships, you can start a new relationship without feelings of inadequacy or self-doubt closing in on you. You can be with your new partner without expecting them to fail in some way. It will be easier for both of you to explore what the limits of the relationship are without any past thoughts getting in the way.

FINDING YOUR FOREVER

There's a big difference between dating someone and deciding that they are going to be your forever. Committing to someone to the point that you're willing to get married and make vows in front of everyone you know and love is an important step. You have to make sure that you're ready to take it. When you are confident, it can be one of the most rewarding feelings in the world.

As you date someone for a while, you may find that you're more comfortable with them than in past relationships. You can open up more, let them in more, and be yourself around them. You don't feel as though there are hundreds of questions swirling around your mind about them. They become your other half, balancing you out in every way.

Before you decide to commit to the forever part, it may be advantageous to sign up for premarital counseling, as Molly did. These are provided by a number of different organizations and individuals. You may find a program at your local church or from a marriage and family therapist. Either way, it can be a great way to make sure that you're on the same page as your partner.

Throughout premarital counseling, you may be asked to take tests away from your partner. This will allow you to answer honestly about topics ranging from careers to kids to finances. Once you both complete the tests, the therapist will look at the answers to see how divided the two of you are on important topics. These will become the talking points that you focus on throughout the different sessions.

Being divided on important topics doesn't mean that you haven't found your forever. It just means that you have some different viewpoints. You need to learn how to talk through these and understand the differences. It's best to do this prior to walking down the aisle simply so that it's already out in the open. If big differences come out a year or two into the marriage, it can cause a breakdown in communication or a constant topic to argue about.

By going through premarital counseling, you learn about each other, what each of you need to thrive, as well as how to communicate effectively. It ensures that you're not only compatible but have the tools necessary to have a happy, healthy relationship until death do you part.

No one can dictate what your forever looks like. No one can dictate when it's time to commit to your forever, either. Be honest with yourself. Self-reflect about the relationship to see how the person makes you feel on every level. If there are red flags, take the time to discover what they are and how they make you feel.

Talk to your friends and family members. If they feel as though you're not seeing the whole picture, take some more time. There should never be a reason to rush into something. If it's right, it will still be right a week from now, a month from now, or even a year from now.

In the end, you deserve happiness. Regardless of what you have been through in the past, you deserve to be loved. You are worthy of being loved. Your happily ever after is right around the corner. You just have to be open to it when it's standing in front of you.

ABOUT THE AUTHOR

Alexandra Hoffman is a hopeless romantic. She always finds the best in every situation, which is also why she has chosen the path of being a life coach and relationship counselor. She lives in Berlin with her husband and three kids, where she has most certainly found her happily ever after.

She didn't find love easily. In fact, she found it the hardest way possible. She has experienced the roller coaster of emotions that comes with the territory of dating the wrong people. It's one of the reasons why she was so motivated to become an author. She is determined to help as many people as possible, and a book is a great way to do that.

Alexandra has helped a number of her friends and her clients find their happily ever after. She takes the time to get down to the root problem so that they understand what's standing in the way of chasing happiness. She feels that once she can expose the root problem, whether it's self-doubt, feelings of inadequacy, or something else, it's easier to overcome those problems and focus on finding a positive relationship.

While Alexandra is the first to admit that no one needs to have a partner in their life, it's often nicer when there is one. It's nice to share life with someone, especially when that person is perfectly balanced. Alexandra and her husband have been married for over 10 years, yet they're still as madly in love as they were on their wedding day. She claims that the secret is to continue dating. The two of them take turns planning dates all across Berlin in order to outdo the other one. Their kids find their kissing "gross" but they'll learn that it's all a sign that their parents have an unbreakable bond. That bond is what Alexandra hopes everyone can find.

Made in the USA
Monee, IL
10 January 2021